STAB IN THE BACK

During a country weekend at the home of a
television celebrity, a brash young comedian
runs into an act that's a real killer: He's
stabbed to death. Now it's up to Detective
Inspector Neil Lambert, a top-notch
mystery solver as well as part-time mystery
writer, to decide who hated the comic
enough to ring down the curtain . . .
forever. It all starts at TV star Logan
Chester's country home. This particular
weekend, however, Chester's orchestrated
a get-together with an unlikely group—
bound only by their hatred of comedian
Tommy Boston.

Books by Malcolm Gray
in the Linford Mystery Library:

LOOK BACK ON MURDER
STAB IN THE BACK

MALCOLM GRAY

STAB IN THE BACK

Complete and Unabridged

LINFORD
Leicester

First Linford Mystery Edition
published March 1989

British Library CIP Data

Gray, Malcolm, *1927*–
    Stab in the back.—Large print ed.—
Linford mystery library
I. Title
823'.914[F]

ISBN 0-7089-6638-1

Published by
F. A. Thorpe (Publishing) Ltd.
Anstey, Leicestershire
Set by Rowland Phototypesetting Ltd.
Bury St. Edmunds, Suffolk
Printed and bound in Great Britain by
T. J. Press (Padstow) Ltd., Padstow, Cornwall

1

ELSIE HEMMINGS dragged herself wearily up the hill. It was only a gentle incline, hardly a hill at all, but the afternoon was warm and her feet hurt. The bunion on the right one was the worst offender: it seemed to set her whole foot on fire where it pressed against her shoe. Elsie was wearing her oldest, most comfortable shoes, stretched and cracked by years of wear and countless other bunions, but it didn't seem to make much difference; every time she put her foot to the ground it was like red-hot knives plunging into her flesh. If it still hurt tomorrow she'd go and see that foot woman over at Wittenham where Gladys Simpkins went. Maybe she'd be able to do something on the National Health.

Pain, Elsie knew, was an affliction intended by God to test poor weak mortals, and it would never have occurred to her to question His ways. All the same, it did seem a little hard it was her who had bad feet and not Millie.

Millie was her younger sister, and Elsie

remembered their mother saying more than once, "Wearing them silly shoes! It's a wonder to me you don't break an ankle. You'll get bunions when you're older. And corns. You'll be sorry then. And all that makeup! You'll be painting your finger-nails next." In Mrs. Hemmings' book painted finger-nails were nearly as bad as dyed hair.

And Millie had. She had gone blond, too, tripping gaily into marriage with Norman Denney, whose father owned the big grocer's at Wittenham. Mrs. Hastings had had dire misgivings about the marriage, but it had prospered, and now, at forty-seven, with a devoted husband and two husky sons who spoilt her, Millie still looked no more than thirty-five.

Elsie, on the other hand, had always done what her mother said, regarding the old lady's prejudices almost as Holy Writ, and although she liked her job as Mr. Chester's "daily" and took a pride in her work, there hadn't been a lot of light and fun in her life. She wasn't conscious of being sorry for herself now, for self-pity was a failing Mrs. Hemmings had never countenanced in others. Virtue, she was fond of saying, was its own reward. It had to be, Elsie reflected with unaccustomed dryness as she passed Mrs. Fenwick's cottage.

Apart from a solitary wisp of cloud the sky was an unbroken blue. July was not yet sufficiently advanced for the trees shading the green to have lost their freshness, but a warm somnolence had settled on the village. A blackbird was singing from the top of an apple tree behind the cottage and Elsie could smell the fragrance of the roses. Mrs. Fenwick was an enthusiastic gardener.

An American visitor had once been heard to exclaim that she guessed Frewley Green was a *real* English village. If by real she meant typical, she was wrong. How many villages, even in England, comprise, besides a fourteenth-century church, a former priory long since reduced to more manageable proportions and converted into a private house; three or four attractive Queen Anne and Georgian homes; forty or fifty cottages, none less than 150 years old, grouped round a green shaded by horse-chestnut trees; an inn nearly as old as the church; a clear stream spanned by a bridge even more ancient; and nothing else? Or almost nothing.

By a combination of good fortune and the

implacable opposition of successive generations of Masterses, major roads bypassed Frewley Green and only the most determined tourists penetrated the maze of lanes which constituted its outer defences. (The American lady was very determined, coming from Chicago and having ancestors born in the village. Also, she was devoted to those detective stories set in improbably picturesque and cosy English villages.) For the most part, the impositions of governments aside, Frewley Green was left pretty much to itself. Life, you might have been forgiven for thinking, like the main roads, passed it by.

It didn't, of course. But one feature of modern life common to less fortunate places did: crime there was almost nonexistent. Nobody counted as a crime Bill Bartlow's poaching Colonel Masters' rabbits and, once or twice a year on special occasions, a pheasant. Not even the colonel. It was part of the rich tapestry of English country life he valued above almost everything else. Anyway, he had no use for his rabbits and more than enough pheasants. He would gladly have given Bartlow a brace if the old boy had asked, but it was more fun for them both for him to poach them.

No ugly rows of council houses marred the

view from the church porch because Colonel Masters had served on the council since 1947 and his father for thirty years before him and they had convinced their fellow councillors that nobody at Frewley Green wanted council houses there. As the council's financial resources were limited and other places were crying out for houses, they met with little opposition. True, one or two left-wingers from the towns muttered darkly about feudal landlords and ignoring democratic procedures, but they were voices crying in the wilderness. In any case they were wrong; the colonel, like his father before him, spoke for nearly everyone in the village. Council houses would have meant new people moving in and change. Frewley Green didn't like change, it preferred life to roll along placidly as it had always done. Change meant upheaval and adapting to new circumstances—and what was new was rarely, in the opinion of Frewley Green, better.

Most of the village families had lived there for generations. The Rayments, who had kept the post office-cum-general store for forty years since Alec Rayment was demobbed from the Army in 1946, were still regarded as new-comers. Nevertheless inevitably there had been changes; old families had died out or the younger generation had moved away, and the people who had taken their places came from towns, attracted by the dream of living in one of the most picturesque villages in England. They didn't belong.

Take her employer, Elsie thought. Logan Chester, he called himself. Silly put-on sort of name, if you asked her. But what could you expect of somebody with his own programme on television? Elsie hardly ever watched television and held a poor opinion of nearly everybody associated with it except Richard Baker, whom she loved. Now he no longer read the nine-o'clock news she watched even less.

Logan Chester had lived at Forge Cottage less than a year. Not that you could really say *lived*: most of the time he was away in London making his programmes or at that college where he was a teacher or something. Still she couldn't complain, he was a good employer and he treated her well.

Forge Cottage had been formed out of three farm-workers' dwellings more than a hundred years ago. At some time during the last century one of its owners had acquired a piece of the adjoining land, and now it stood, an attractively uneven timberframed building with white walls and a tiled roof, in over an acre of garden and orchard. Beyond it houses of varying ages and sizes climbed the slope towards the church and looked across the green to the Wheatsheaf and the old school, now a cottage where old Miss Haythorne lived with her two West Highland terriers and her memories. Mostly the memories were of hot, lazy afternoons, tea on the veranda brought by dark-skinned servants and balls at which she had worn lovely gowns. Miss Haythorne's father had been a major in the Indian Army in the halcyon days before 1939.

Beyond the church the road passed the gates of Frewley Priory, where Masterses had lived for nearly three hundred years, and turned right, crossing the tiny River Frew by the humpbacked bridge which was only wide enough to accommodate one car at a time, and that with difficulty.

A little way up the road a small, bright red car was parked outside one of the houses. As Elsie was about to turn in at the gate of Forge Cottage a young woman came out of the front door laughing gaily and got into it. Whatever the condition of her feet there was nothing wrong with Elsie's eyes, and she could see that the girl was strikingly attractive. (If you care for that sort of looks, she added in her own mind.) For with her silver-blond hair swinging round her shoulders, her make-up and her flame-coloured dress the girl looked as out of place in Frewley Green as an exotic, vividly hued bird in an English hedgerow. She started the car and drove off towards the bend at the top of the hill.

Taking her time, Elsie made her way round to the rear of Forge Cottage and let herself in by the back door. The kitchen was a light, airy room, and after the heat outside the atmosphere seemed distinctly cool. Elsie permitted herself a sigh of pleasure as she took out the slippers she kept in a cupboard and savoured the exquisite relief of removing her shoes. Then, tying on an apron, she set about preparing the vegetables for Logan Chester's supper. For Elsie dinner was the meal you ate in the middle of the day; anything after six o'clock was supper.

The range and luxury of the kitchen's new fittings never failed to amaze and delight her. The cabinets lining two of the walls were good enough for a bedroom. And *three* stainless steel sinks! When she thought what it had been like when old Mr. and Mrs. Foster lived in the cottage words failed her. But then, she hadn't realized how old-fashioned and inconvenient everything was any more than they had. She didn't dare think what it must have cost to put in all these things. But although she felt that she should disapprove of such extravagance, she loved her kitchen. Even the old scullery had been converted into a utility-room with a freezer and an automatic washing-machine.

Mr. Chester didn't mind spending money, she'd say that for him. A bit too freely in her opinion, and that of most of the village; Frewley Green didn't approve of people who put their money about too lavishly. It upset the proper order of things.

She was preparing the new potatoes when Susan Wareham put her head round the door.

"Can I come in?" she asked.

The kitchen was Elsie's domain and when she was there Susan always obtained her permission before entering it, a fact which Elsie noted and appreciated. She approved of Logan Chester's secretary.

Susan was twenty-eight and single. She didn't consider herself pretty, and she wasn't in a conventional way, but she had nice dark hair which she kept fairly short and simply styled and fine grey eyes. Her clothes were always neat and suited her, and she spent rather a lot of her salary on them.

"There'll be three people staying this weekend and four more counting me coming for the day on Saturday," she said now. "I'm sorry it's rather short notice, but I thought Mr. Chester had told you."

"'S the first I've 'eard of it," Elsie said.

"Oh dear, it's my fault. He'll cook dinner tomorrow night and Saturday and we'll have something cold with a salad for Saturday lunch. Do you think you could get most of the salad things ready and leave them in the fridge?" Susan asked.

"That's all right, miss," Elsie assured her.

It would mean a little extra work, but she didn't mind that. Never had. Chester hardly ever ventured into the kitchen when she was in occupation but, according to what he said, he was an expert cook. All that fancy stuff, sauces and what have you, Elsie supposed. Her idea of proper food was a joint and two veg and a steamed suet pudding after.

When he bought the cottage and she agreed to stay on to work for him, Chester had asked her what he should call her, fully expecting her to tell him her name was Rose or Dora or something he would consider suited her as well. Instead she had replied calmly and politely, "My name's 'Emmings, sir. Miss 'Emmings." Which Chester already knew. He was sufficiently abashed never to make the experiment of calling her anything else. Nor was he ever overbearing with Elsie, whom he both liked and respected, although she would have been very surprised if anybody had told her so. Susan, on the other hand, always called her by her Christian name, something which Elsie considered perfectly correct.

"Would it 'elp if I came in for a bit on Saturday, to clear away an' that?" she enquired now. She would rather come, there would be enough mess to clear up on Monday as it was, if past experience was anything to go by. Mr. Chester might be a good cook; he wasn't so expert at clearing up afterwards.

"Oh, if you could," Susan said gratefully. "But if it's not convenient we can manage."

"That'll be all right, miss," Elsie assured her.

"Thank you very much," Susan said.

She returned to the study, where Chester was waiting to dictate some more letters. He was forty, a burly man with untidy brown hair and

11

heavy features. His lower lip was full enough to give his mouth a slightly sensual look and self-indulgence had thickened his figure, but many women found him attractive. Two years ago he had been an unknown and undistinguished academic, a junior lecturer in the English department at one of the more obscure provincial universities, when at a dinner party he had met a television producer. The producer had thought him an opinionated, egotistical bore, and when a few weeks later one of his colleagues was stuck at short notice for a member of a panel for a quiz programme he had remembered him.

"Logan Chester? I've never heard of him," the colleague objected. "Nor has anybody else."

"They soon will have if you use him properly," Chester's acquaintance told him. "He's ideal material for your stuff, bumptious, ill-mannered, lays down the law about everything. And he has some sort of accent—Northumberland, I believe. He makes rather a thing of it so it's probably put on. What more could you want?"

"Oh Gawd!"

"Just have a look at him, Richard. See if I'm not right."

Having no alternative in view and very little time, the producer did, and within two minutes of their meeting he was reassured. Colin was right; except that his manners weren't really bad, Chester was everything he had said. The man was a television natural.

From the day his first programme went out Chester had gone from strength to strength. He taught even less than before, and in two years had written three books, two of which had already been published. One was a study of crime fiction since 1945, a subject on which he was an authority and on which he had lectured at an American university, the other an account, part fact more fiction, of his time in the USA. Nine months ago he had been given his own television programme, a hotchpotch of interviews, comment and opinions, principally his own. Now he was frequently commissioned by the "quality" papers to write articles and express views on subjects about which he knew next to nothing. He was invited to dinner by people he didn't know, and requests poured in for him to speak at lunches and dinners. Logan Chester was a celebrity, and he loved it.

"What's the matter, darling?" Cicely Robins asked gently.

Her daughter looked up. "Matter?" she repeated. "Nothing's the matter. Why should it be?"

"Don't be silly, Gill. A blind person could see there's something. If you don't want to tell me what it is, don't. But if you do, or if you think I can help . . ."

Gillian didn't answer at once. Then she muttered, "I don't know what it is."

Her mother regarded her with a concern not wholly unmixed with amusement. If Gill really didn't know, and Cicely found that hard to believe, it was clear enough to her. But it wasn't really funny.

Gill was a lovely woman, she thought. Her dark brown hair had red lights in it, her features were small enough without being too small and her large grey eyes were thickly fringed with lashes. She had always been beautiful, even as a child. Now, at thirty-two, her beauty had matured.

If Gill wouldn't acknowledge what was wrong, there was nothing she could do. She hoped devoutly her daughter wouldn't do anything silly and start talking about a divorce. She could be infuriatingly headstrong at times.

But this trouble between her and Trevor couldn't be serious, could it?

Not for the first time Cicely wondered what it was had attracted Gill to him in the first place. Was it his vitality, his determination to achieve what he wanted, to make his business a success and live in a style his parents had never dreamed of? Or was it his looks, his strong body and fair hair and laughing blue eyes? Cicely could see their attractions. But perhaps she was doing Gill an injustice and she had seen that under his brash manner there was kindness and strength of character.

Now Trevor wanted children and she didn't. Or thought she didn't; Cicely refused to believe a daughter of hers could really not want a family. Poor Trevor, she thought. She was very fond of her son-in-law and sometimes Gill's attitude to him annoyed her intensely.

"It's tomorrow," Gill said. "I wish now I hadn't said we'd go."

"I thought you were looking forward to it," Cicely commented. "Is it Trevor?"

"Oh, he doesn't want to. He's being too boring about the whole thing."

"And now you don't know whether you do or not."

"I *do*. Alethea Wightman's going to be there, Logan's publisher. I told you. He thinks she's going to say she'll take my book."

"So what are you worried about?"

"Nothing," Gillian muttered, avoiding her mother's eye.

There was a brief silence, then Cicely said calmly, "You've been seeing quite a lot of Logan Chester lately, haven't you?"

"No." Gillian spoke a little louder than was necessary. As if she realized it she added more quietly, "Not really. It's only because of the book."

"Do you like him?"

"He's clever and amusing, and he knows a lot of interesting people."

"That's not an answer," Cicely observed.

"All right," Gill said with a hint of defiance that told her mother her conscience was not quite easy. "Yes, I like him."

Oh dear! Cicely thought. One of her worst fears seemed to be well founded: Gill was either considering having an affair with Logan Chester or was already having one. That was why she was so evasive and restless now; she was unhappy because she was uncertain and felt guilty and didn't like herself very much. Cicely

16

was convinced that despite everything Gill still loved her husband. She had seen very little of Chester, but what she had seen she hadn't liked at all.

"If I were you, I wouldn't go," she said.

"But I must see Alethea Wightman."

"Couldn't you go to her office? Or ask her here?"

"I don't suppose she'd come; Logan said he had to work hard to persuade her to stay this weekend. He's taken a lot of trouble."

"Then you should go," Cicely said calmly. "You'd be letting him down very badly if you didn't."

"I was going to," Gillian told her, and went out.

Cicely heard her walking back down the passage to the main part of the house, which she and Trevor occupied. The house was all theirs, and it occurred to Cicely for the first time that if worse came to worst and they split up, she would have to leave her flat. She wouldn't like that, she was very happy here.

"Tommy Boston!" Susan exclaimed. "You haven't asked *him*? You can't!"

"Why not?" Chester demanded, amused by

her vehemence and at the same time mildly irritated. He disliked having his judgement questioned and being told he couldn't do anything.

"That's just it, why?" Susan asked brutally. "After how he behaved when you had him on your programme."

"I don't bear him any malice for that."

"You did at the time."

Chester grinned. "Time's a great healer, as somebody once said. Who was it?"

"I've no idea." Susan bit back the retort which had sprung to her lips. She knew her employer well enough to understand he was deliberately changing the subject to put her off, and this time she had no intention of being sidetracked. She felt too strongly. "He's a terrible man," she said. "Really terrible. You don't know. He should be locked away."

Chester regarded her curiously; it was unlike Susan to become so worked up about anything. "You must know something about him I don't," he observed. "What is it?"

2

"WHAT a charming house," Alethea Wightman commented, looking round at the white walls, the genuine oak beams and the carefully chosen furniture which suited them so well. Despite her habitual vagueness her tone succeeded in blending approval and condescension in equal measures, hinting subtly that the effect Chester had achieved was the result of luck rather than his good taste. Or, perhaps, the taste of the previous owner. Alethea had no intention of giving him the satisfaction of having her praise anything of his too highly.

To herself she was prepared to admit she was surprised. When she saw Forge Cottage from the road she had feared the worst, fully expecting that inside Chester would have indulged in a frenzy of olde worldeliness, turning a rather delightful house into a travesty of Merrie England. That he hadn't she found mildly disappointing. It was as though he had scored a point in some unspoken contest between them, and Alethea hadn't believed him capable of surprising her—unless it was by some new manifestation of bad taste.

"I'm so glad you like it," Chester said, smiling a trifle smugly. He wasn't a fool in many things and he knew Alethea well enough to read her thoughts fairly accurately. She couldn't feel superior about his house, and that disconcerted her; Alethea had to feel superior about everything, from the soap in her bathroom to her judgement of books. It was almost her *raison d'être*.

She was not only Chester's editor, she was also a director of the firm which had already published two of his books and would shortly publish the third; she was a tall, very thin woman with a long, pale face and hair twisted into an untidy bun. The long, limp dresses she affected—most things about Alethea were affected rather than merely worn or assumed—accentuated her appearance of languor with their pale greys and mauves. She made Chester think of a very anaemic stick of asparagus which had been left out too long and gone limp.

She had disliked his so-called American diary intensely, but appreciated that with all the publicity he received—and which cost her firm nothing—the book would inevitably sell tens of thousands of copies in hardback and, later, many more thousands in paperback. The prospect of his features leering at her from every newspaper and bookstall appalled her, but, however much they might regret and try to deny it, even publishers had to take a mercenary view sometimes, and for the time being he was a valuable property. She preferred to think of him like that rather than as a human being, and she comforted herself with the knowledge that it wouldn't be for long; Logan Chester was one of that strange, transient breed whose faces became as familiar to the world at large as the prime minister's for a time, then disappeared and were forgotten as new celebrities came along to usurp their places. In the meantime she disliked him with all the bitter resentment of one supreme egotist for another.

She had accepted his invitation to spend this weekend at Forge Cottage partly because the prospect of two days in her cramped London flat in a heat-wave filled her with dismay, and partly because of the typescript he had sent her a month ago. He had told her nothing about the author, but she took it for granted she was, or would shortly be, one of his succession of mistresses. Alethea doubted whether that band was as numerous as he liked to hint. And how any woman could . . . Ughh!

When she received the novel she had breathed a faint sigh of resignation and sent it to the least impressionable of her readers. To her surprise the reader had been enthusiastic, and the second to whom she sent it was equally impressed. Alethea had then read the book herself and liked it. When Chester told her the author would be among his guests this weekend —had he understood she would need an incentive to persuade her to come? she wondered— she had decided to accept his invitation, although not without misgivings. She wanted that book, and she wouldn't put it past Logan to offer it to another publisher behind her back. Meeting the author would be some sort of insurance. For that she was prepared to endure a weekend at Forge Cottage.

Alethea didn't drive and she had caught a train which arrived at Wittenham at ten minutes past four. Chester had met her there in his big old black Austin, a car he loved. It had done yeoman service for many years with the mayors of a small Midlands town before he bought it at an auction, and he believed that in some way it enhanced his image. Alethea felt hot and grimy and she wanted only to freshen up in readiness for the ordeal she was convinced lay ahead. First, however, her host was determined to show off the rest of his house. She sighed and hoped devoutly he wouldn't want her to accompany him on a conducted tour of the garden as well. It looked large, and gardens, in her opinion, should be admired from a distance, not explored.

When they entered the house by the front door the dining-room with one of its two doors had been on their right and Chester's study on their left. The hall formed a T, with the kitchen, the utility-room and a cloakroom on the other side of the long horizontal. The drawing-room, to which he had taken her first, comprised the whole ground floor of one of the original cottages and extended the depth of that end of the house. The stairs went up just outside the door, across the hall from the other door of the dining-room.

Alethea followed Chester into the study. It was a fair-sized room with bookshelves lining two of the walls and part of a third. Apart from a big mahogany desk with an upright chair behind it, the only furniture consisted of two easy chairs, a standard lamp and, in one corner, a steel filing cabinet. Alethea wondered why the room should immediately call to her mind the description masculine merely because of the desk and the books. Many women would be as much at home there as any man. She would herself.

"Who else is coming?" she enquired.

"Your new author and her husband," Chester replied.

"You take it for granted we'll publish her book?" The words seemed to float from Alethea's lips, suggesting the matter was by no means decided and was of little interest to her anyway.

"You know damned well you will," her host told her. "They're coming tomorrow with Peter Hastings. You know him, don't you?"

"Hardly."

"He lives in the village. Tommy Boston and his wife are staying for the weekend. They should be here anytime."

Alethea stared at him. She was both startled and shocked. "You're not serious. I don't believe it, even of you."

"Believe what?" Chester asked innocently.

"That you'd invite that man. He's repulsive."
Alethea was so put out her languid manner
almost deserted her.

"Boston, you mean?" Chester grinned again.
"I know he's not everybody's cup of tea,
but—"

"He's loathsome."

"You published his autobiography."

"We publish a lot of books by people we
don't like," Alethea said unpleasantly. She
didn't care if she offended Logan; her firm had
an option on his next book, and by the time it
was published his star would almost certainly
be waning. The prospect of his being ignored
and forgotten pleased her. He had known very
well how she felt about that horrible little so-
called comedian, she remembered telling him
when he'd had Boston on his programme three
or four months ago, yet he had deliberately
invited him here for the same weekend as her.

And why invite him at all after Boston had
set out to make him look a fool on that programme? As for his wife—was she his fourth
or his fifth?—the dancer he had married last
year in a blaze of publicity the day after
divorcing her predecessor, Alethea could guess
what she would be like. This weekend, she told

herself, was going to be even worse than she had anticipated.

"I would like to wash," she said coldly. "The train was filthy."

"Yes, of course," Chester agreed, his tone more conciliatory. Picking up her case, he led the way upstairs.

As he came down again a few minutes later a car drew up beside the house and he went to the front door. Tommy Boston and his wife were getting out of a sky-blue Rolls-Royce. The comedian was a short, thick-set man in his middle fifties. His balding scalp was partly concealed by a hair-piece and his rather protuberant eyes by heavy rimmed glasses. With his casual jacket and trousers that matched the car went rather pointed brown boots, a pink shirt open at the neck and a heavy gold chain bracelet. There were dark sweat patches under both armpits of his jacket.

Carole Boston was twenty-four and slim and with her long shining blond hair and make-up looked exactly like one of her frequent pictures in *TV Times*. She was wearing a white shirt with primrose-yellow cotton trousers which showed off the length of her dancer's legs and white sandals. Even without her high heels she was a good three inches taller than her husband.

"It's lovely," she exclaimed delightedly, looking at the house. "Isn't it, Tommy?"

Boston, lugging a heavy case from the car, merely grunted. He had put on a good deal of weight over the last year or two and exertion of any sort left him breathless. Locking the car, he straightened up and started towards Chester, who had come out of the house to welcome them. Carole followed.

Dinner that evening was an uncomfortable meal. Alethea had heard of comedians who, away from their work, were quiet, unassuming men. Boston wasn't one of them. It seemed that the personality he presented on-stage, brash, vulgar and aggressive, was the real man. He employed towards his companions at the table the same hectoring manner he used to his audiences. Moreover from the time they gathered for drinks in the drawing-room before dinner, right through the meal, he told a succession of stories which Alethea, who, while fastidious, was no prude, found thoroughly distasteful. To make it worse, he told them much too loudly in his stage-Cockney accent.

Even Chester, who was usually capable of quelling anybody, seemed powerless to stop him. Perhaps, Alethea thought, he didn't want to. It was even possible he was enjoying the stories. Or more likely, she told herself bitterly, he was enjoying their effect on her. She retreated into her own thoughts, emerging only when one of the others addressed her directly.

Carole Boston was just as unhappy, although for different reasons, and, unlike Alethea, she didn't know how to ignore what was happening. She had heard all Tommy's ghastly stories time and time again before. Why didn't he stop? Surely he could see the Wightman woman was absolutely furious. But he didn't seem to care. Nor did Logan Chester.

Carole decided she didn't like Logan very much. He made her uneasy. No, apprehensive, that was the word. It was silly, why should she be afraid of an overweight, conceited man who had made a name for himself by being rude about people and things on television? He had been very sarcastic about the programme in which she was one of the hostesses. She didn't mind that much, although it seemed a bit pointless when the show wasn't meant for people like him and millions of others enjoyed it. But what had he ever done?

"There was this little darling," Boston was saying, beginning yet another story. "Proper cracker she was. You know, ev'rything 'ere and there. And 'ere." He leered at Alethea, who was thinking about some new curtains for her flat and didn't see him. "Well, one day she met this bloody great coon."

He went on and on. There must be some way of having her revenge, Alethea told herself. He was inordinately proud of his autobiography; she would say something really disparaging about that. It wouldn't be difficult.

Usually the memoirs of sportsmen and show-business stars were "ghosted" by authors who specialized in writing books for other people, but Tommy Boston's had been all his own work. He had guaranteed that. And although it hadn't been good, it was certainly much better than she would have thought this oafish moron capable of writing.

Boston came to the end of his story and Logan Chester laughed obligingly. Carole didn't bother.

"A couple who live in the village are coming to lunch tomorrow," Chester said. "Trevor and

Gillian Lane. He used to be a builder, then he started dealing in property and doing a bit of development."

"Trevor Lane?" Boston said.

"Yes. Do you know him?"

"No, never met 'im. No connection of Penny Lane, is 'e?"

"Not that I know." Chester smiled amiably. "Gill's written a novel. It's very good and Alethea wanted to meet her. And a chap called Peter Hastings is coming. Do you know him, Tommy?"

Carole was watching her husband.

"Never 'eard of 'im," Boston said in his loud voice. "I thought 'Astings was a place, not a person. What's 'is cousin called? Eastbourne?"

"No, Lewes," Chester replied.

"Lewes. That's good." Boston laughed noisily.

It was unusual for him to appreciate anybody else's jokes, even such feeble ones, and Chester experienced a small glow of satisfaction. It had showed Tommy was rattled. With luck he would be more than rattled before the weekend was over.

Carole knew Chester was watching her. She felt herself going pale and was glad she had put on more make-up before coming down to dinner. As it was, in the shadowed room with only the light of the candles on the table and the sun sinking behind the trees in the orchard, probably no one would notice. But Logan knew. Goodness knew how he had found out, but somehow he had. Suddenly, uncontrollably, she shivered.

Saturday dawned fine with the promise of being as hot as the previous day. Alethea had taken the precaution of bringing some work with her, and as soon as she could escape from the un-welcome company of her host and his other guests she took some scripts and a deck-chair to a remote corner of the lawn where she was partially screened from the house by a tall clump of rhododendrons.

There she read contentedly for an hour to the accompaniment of a blackbird's singing and the muted sound of the few cars which drove past the house. Pigeons cooed in the wood a couple of hundred yards away and once or twice a cabbage-white butterfly fluttered past her en route for the vegetable garden. Once a frog emerged from some moist foliage, gazed round with its bulging, interested eyes and hopped away. Alethea worked on undisturbed, oblivious of it all. She wasn't an outdoor person, but she would have been prepared to concede that it was much more pleasant there than it would have been indoors. The only drawback was that she would have to rejoin Logan Chester and the others all too soon.

Once she said aloud, "No, it won't do." She was reading the typescript of the new novel by one of her most successful authors. It was nothing like as good as his others, and if it had been written by anybody less well established —and less profitable for her firm—she would have turned it down out of hand. As it was, she supposed they would have to publish it or risk losing him. She decided to send him a warning letter, and if his next book showed no improvement . . . Laying the neat pile of paper on one side, she picked up another.

It was Gillian Lane's book. She had resolved to glance through it again to refresh her memory when Chester told her the Lanes were coming this weekend, and she skimmed through it now with the speed of a professional reader. This time she thought she detected in it something she had missed before. Or, rather, something the significance of which had escaped her, because it couldn't be anything Chester had said that had opened her eyes. He had hardly mentioned either of the Lanes, apart from that brief comment at dinner last night.

Alethea turned back several pages and read certain passages again. Then, with a mental shrug, she continued reading from the point she had reached before. It would be interesting to see what Gillian Lane's husband was like, she thought.

She was so engrossed in her work she failed to hear footsteps approaching, and the first she knew of Tommy Boston's presence only a few feet away was when he said, "Oh, so that's where you're 'iding. We can't 'ave you burying yourself away like this, Alethea."

"Why not?" Alethea demanded. She disliked his calling her by her Christian name very much, and she was angry both with him and with herself for allowing him to catch her un-awares.

"Well, it's not very friendly, is it?" Boston came closer. "We all want to be friendly, don't we?"

"Frankly," Alethea told him, "no."

The comedian seemed no whit abashed, and as she started to get up from the deck-chair he put out a hand to help her. Since he was directly in front of her and only a couple of feet away, Alethea had no choice but to take it. Grinning, Boston pulled slightly harder than was necessary, and as she stumbled towards him, slightly off balance, he put out his other arm and embraced her clumsily.

"That's more like it," he said approvingly, aiming a kiss at her neck.

Alethea was furious. She hadn't been exaggerating when she told Chester she found the comedian loathsome, and added to her natural revulsion at having him breathing all over her trying to kiss her was the knowledge that she must look ridiculous. If she had had a knife to hand, she would have stabbed him without compunction. As she hadn't, she made do with the only weapon at her disposal. Opening her clenched teeth, she bit hard into his left ear. The thought of any physical contact with Boston might be repugnant to her; that didn't stop her experiencing a feeling of profound satisfaction as her sharp teeth dug deep into his flesh.

At the same moment she became aware of Logan Chester standing watching them.

Boston yelped and released his hold on her waist. "You bitch!" he muttered.

Alethea was delighted to see that blood was beginning to seep from his ear. She pushed him away, gathered up her things with as much dignity as she could muster and stalked off towards the house, ignoring Chester, who had the temerity to grin.

"Well, well, well," he observed, watching Boston. "Who'd have thought it of you two? I'd no idea our Alethea got up to larks in the bushes."

The comedian, trying to staunch his bleeding ear with his handkerchief, glared at him but said nothing and departed towards the house in Alethea's wake.

3

SUSAN had promised Chester she would arrive about midday, and it was characteristic of her that she drove up in her Metro a few minutes after eleven forty-five. None of the overnight guests was about and she went in search of her employer, who was alone in the drawing-room, still amused by what he had seen in the garden.

The Lanes came twenty minutes later. Trevor, a tall, well-built man with sandy hair thinning at his temples and very blue eyes, was five years older than his wife. Although he was said to be a tough businessman, something about him suggested a boyish vulnerability. At first Gillian had found it irresistible; now she resented it, as if it were a trick he used to give him an unfair advantage.

Chester greeted her with a kiss, which she returned a little too affectionately, and smiled at Trevor. "I'm glad you could both come," he said.

Susan saw that Trevor hadn't wanted to; his

unsmiling nod and abrupt "Hallo" spoke louder than words. She saw, too, that his manner was embarrassing and annoying Gillian, but Chester couldn't care less. He had a skin like a rhinoceros, she thought bitterly. Sometimes in her blacker moments she wondered if he cared at all about people's feelings. It was impossible to tell now how much he was interested in Gillian Lane. If he was interested at all.

Gillian for her part was still unhappy and confused. She wasn't by nature promiscuous, and while she liked Chester and was grateful for his help over her book, she couldn't deceive herself there was anything more to it. Also she was honest enough with herself to acknowledge that a large part of his attraction was his fame and the people he knew. If she had an affair with him, it would be primarily because she wanted to revenge herself on Trevor—and she wasn't sure she wanted that enough to risk destroying their marriage.

Hastings arrived almost on the heels of the Lanes. He was a year or two younger than Trevor, a dark, reserved man a little below average height and slightly built. Watching him, Susan decided he was shy.

When the Bostons appeared, the party had

moved into the drawing-room for drinks before lunch.

"Oh, there you are," Chester greeted them cheerfully. "Repaired the damage, Tommy?"

The comedian glared at him but didn't answer.

Gillian saw that Trevor was gazing at Boston, amazement and anger in his look. It puzzled and vaguely disturbed her.

Alethea had timed her arrival downstairs to be the last on the scene and thus avoid the necessity of talking to Boston. She entered the room while Chester was introducing the other guests to each other. Susan, who had met her before, privately considered her so affected as to be slightly ridiculous, although Chester said she was extremely good at her job. The Bostons were strangers, although she had once seen Tommy from a distance, an occasion she knew she would never be able to forget. Now, by involving herself in a discussion with Alethea and keeping her back turned to Chester, she was able to avoid being introduced to him. From what she could hear, he was everything she had expected him to be. Carole she put down as attractive in an obvious way, probably stupid and almost certainly mercenary. The sort of person, Susan thought, you could dismiss with a mental shrug so long as you didn't have to have much to do with them.

She saw with wry amusement that Logan was looking after the Lanes, more accurately Gillian, and asked Alethea what she would like to drink.

"Oh, a tonic water," Alethea replied, rather as if she should have known.

"By itself?"

"Yes, of course. With a slice of lemon."

As Susan went to fetch it, Boston suddenly said loudly, "We don't want to stay here by ourselves. That looks a nice little pub across the green, why don't we go over there? Eh, Logan?"

The comedian was always happiest in small crowds where he was likely to be recognized— if not, he had perfected ways of making himself known—and he could see he wouldn't get an admiring audience here. The Wightman woman couldn't stick his guts because he'd done her the favour of making a bit of a pass out there in the garden. He'd only done it for a giggle, to cheer her up. 'Strewth, she needed it, miserable-looking cow. And Logan's secretary, looking at him as if he'd brought a bad smell in with him and avoiding speaking to him. He'd let her know what he thought of her. Too damned right he would.

The Lanes were better. If the wife did think she was Lady Muck, her husband looked like he'd rather have a jar with the lads in the pub than sissy drinks in little glasses here.

But most of all Boston wanted to avoid Hastings. More particularly, he wanted to prevent Hastings talking to Alethea Wightman. Boston didn't trust anybody.

He had made his suggestion sound more like a command. Alethea shuddered and wondered how she could decline to go. She decided resentfully she couldn't.

Carole didn't want to go either—Tommy in public embarrassed her even more than with a few "friends"—but none of the others seemed to mind. Except, perhaps, Susan Wareham. Not even Peter. And after all, it might be safer at the pub with people crowding them and too much noise for real conversation.

"You want to go, don't you, my love?" Tommy said, putting an arm round her waist.

"I don't mind," she agreed brightly in the tone she knew he expected of her. She wondered how he had been hurt. He had come

40

up to their room clutching the side of his face, his handkerchief liberally stained with blood. But when she asked him what had happened, he hadn't answered. Had he gone too far and driven Logan to take a swing at him?

But a punch wouldn't have caused all that bleeding, would it? And they seemed friendly enough now. All the same, something had happened. One of these days, if he didn't watch his tongue and keep his hands to himself, Tommy would go too far. Then he'd better look out.

Trevor was only too glad to go to the Wheatsheaf. He would feel more at home there than here with people with whom he had nothing in common. Peter Hastings was all right, and Logan's secretary, too, but the others . . . He couldn't think why Gill had been so keen to come. She'd said it was something to do with that book she'd been writing for the past year, but he hadn't taken that much notice. She couldn't enjoy being with this lot, surely?

Gillian wondered how, if they went to the pub, she could manoeuvre a few minutes' private conversation with Alethea, who wasn't at all what she had expected. For all the older woman's vagueness, Gillian found her rather intimidating. Most likely she hadn't read her book, and if she had she wouldn't want to talk about it here. Probably she hadn't liked it and would be embarrassed if it were mentioned. Not that she looked as if she could be embarrassed that easily; more likely she would put Gillian firmly in her place. Perhaps it would be best if they went to the pub.

They went, Chester putting his head round the kitchen door to say, "We're going across to the pub, Miss Hemmings. We'll be back in twenty minutes."

"Very good, sir," Elsie said. I'll believe that when I see it, she thought.

She was not, therefore, at all surprised when it was nearly three quarters of an hour before the party returned, but she shook her head disapprovingly as she put the final touches to the salad.

When she took lunch into the dining-room they were already sitting round the table, and it was clear the oldest of the men, the squat, flashy one Mr. Chester called Tommy, had had more than enough to drink. Mr. Lane and Mr. Chester himself seemed cheerful and quite sober, but none of the women looked as if they

42

were enjoying themselves much. Not even Mrs. Boston. It had given Elsie quite a start when she saw Carole this morning.

She put down the last of the dishes and went out, closing the door behind her.

"That one looks sour enough to turn the cream," Boston observed without waiting for it to shut.

Elsie heard him.

"She's wonderful," Chester protested, picking up a bottle and starting to pour the wine. "I won't have you say a word against her."

But Boston was not to be stopped. "I'd 'ave thought you could do better than 'er," he said. "A bachelor living on 'is own like you do. Coo. Couldn't you find one with a bit more of what it takes, eh?"

"For heaven's sake shut up," Carole told him fiercely. "Not everybody's like you. And not everybody thinks talking like that's very amusing."

Alethea regarded her with interest.

Good for Carole, Susan thought. She wouldn't have believed she had it in her. The blond girl went up in her estimation.

Poor Logan, Gillian said to herself. Though he didn't look concerned.

Boston was glaring at his wife. "You want to remember what you are, doll," he growled. The threat, unspecific as it was, was all too clear, but Carole seemed untroubled.

There was an embarrassed silence, broken by Alethea turning to Gillian and saying in her remote voice, "I've read your book, Mrs. Lane."

"Oh, have you?" Gillian's heart beat a little faster. This was what she had been waiting for, wondering how to bring it about, and now it had come without her having had anything to do with it, it seemed almost an anticlimax because of the foul man on her left. She waited nervously for what Alethea might say.

"I think we may be able to take it on," the older woman told her vaguely. "There are two or three things will need looking at, but . . ." The sentence trailed away.

Gillian was overjoyed. She had hardly dared dream of this, it was one of the great moments of her life. Yet underlying her elation was a secret fear. If—now she could almost say to herself when—her book was published, would people who read it draw their own conclusions?

44

For however much she might protest she had used her marriage only as a basis for a story that was all fiction, there was too much of them both in it for a denial to carry conviction.

Perhaps it wasn't too late even now to alter it so that they wouldn't connect the principal characters with Trevor and her. After all, Alethea Wightman had said there were things that would need attention. And if it couldn't be changed? Was she prepared to see it remain unpublished, a dream gathering dust in a cupboard, rather than face the consequences? You've got to face it, she told herself, which is more important to you, the book or your marriage?

When she started the book she had thought only vaguely of its being published. She had written a few articles before, and it had been both an escape and something she could achieve on her own. It shocked her now to realize that partly it had been a substitute child. It was only later, as she became more and more involved with it and the characters, she began to take it really seriously. By then it was too late.

While sometimes she might resent or be hurt by Trevor's lack of interest, she had depended on it. He had shown so little interest when she told him what she was doing that eventually she had stopped saying anything. But when it was published people who knew them would read it and some were bound to start asking questions. Trevor would learn then. Almost she wished she hadn't allowed Logan to send it to Alethea.

"It's not bad," Tommy Boston declared in a tone of qualified approval. Perhaps he thought it was time he re-established himself in the party's good graces.

Gillian frowned and Alethea regarded him with loathing. "What isn't?" she demanded icily.

"Gill's book. Not for a first effort. It is your first, isn't it, love?" His breath, loaded with alcohol, fanned Gillian's cheek and she turned her head away. "They say people always put themselves into their first books. Did you know that? Do you reckon anybody's going to recognize you?"

Gillian was horrified. "You've read it?" she asked incredulously.

But Boston had achieved his purpose, the others were eyeing him with interest, and he was too cunning to commit himself. "Mind you," he said, "a novel's different to a proper book. When you're writing about real life you 'ave to do all the research. You 'ave to 'ave your facts right, an' that takes time. Not that I mind. I remember when my first book came out . . ."

They stared at him in astonishment. Gillian, looking across the table, was startled to see Peter Hastings' expression. He looked as if he would like to strangle Boston, she thought. For a moment his expression frightened her and she wondered what he was really like behind his quiet, diffident manner. Then he turned and she saw he was smiling faintly and she wondered if perhaps she had imagined the murderous look in his eyes. That it had been only a trick of the light.

"Have you written many books?" he asked.

"One or two." The comedian managed to give the impression of a proper modesty, and that in fact he had written more. "I had my autobiography out last winter, didn't I, Alethea? Her firm published it. It hasn't sold too badly, has it? Not badly at all. But I wasn't happy with it."

"Oh?" Hastings said.

"It was badly written." Boston smiled. "I'd know better next time."

"More wine?" Chester asked.

Gillian saw he was addressing her. "No,

thank you," she said. She was suddenly conscious of something pressing her left thigh and realized to her astonishment it was Tommy Boston's hand. If it hadn't been so unwelcome it would have been funny, she thought. Who did the unsavoury little toad think he was? First he was patronizing about her book, now he was making a pass at her under the table. Controlling her anger with difficulty, she turned to him and asked in a clear voice, "Do you want us to go to bed now, Tommy, or shall we wait until after lunch?"

There was a stunned silence. Boston, who had gone redder than ever, spluttered. Chester, after a second when he looked as if he couldn't believe his ears, burst out laughing, apparently deciding that was the best way of handling the situation. Alethea had retreated into her own thoughts when Boston started talking about his books and seemed unaware of what was happening. The others were gazing in astonishment at Gillian.

Except Trevor, who was seated opposite her. In him bewilderment struggled with fury. It was unlike Gillian to come out with something like that, even as a joke. He could hardly believe she'd said it. "What the hell do you mean?" he demanded.

Gillian was surprised how calm and in control of the situation she felt. "From what Tommy was doing under the table, I assumed that was what he wanted," she explained. "After all, that sort of thing is rather in his line, isn't it?"

Boston's embarrassment had turned to anger. "Look," he said thickly, "if you think, just because I may have touched your leg by accident, I want—"

"What?" Trevor demanded angrily.

"I didn't even know I'd touched 'er."

"Didn't you?" Gillian asked sweetly. "That wasn't the impression I got. I mean, you—"

"I tell you, it was an accident," Boston nearly shouted. "What's all the fuss about?"

"You're drunk," Carole told him disgustedly. She seemed on the verge of tears.

"Come on," Chester said with a brave attempt at joviality. The situation was rapidly getting out of hand. "It was a misunderstanding. All right, Gill?"

"Like hell it was," Trevor retorted.

"I tell you, I didn't mean anything," Boston pleaded. He knew they were all against him and

49

he had faced too many hostile audiences in the past not to see when he was beaten. "If Gill thought I did, I'm sorry. What more can I say?"

"That's all right then. Eh, Gill?" Chester said hopefully.

"I suppose so," Gillian agreed. Her tone made it clear she knew she had won and she was giving nothing away.

"There were some passages seemed to me very true to life," Alethea remarked. The others, relieved that what looked like becoming an unpleasant scene had been averted, gaped at her. It seemed she had heard nothing of what was going on. "The relationship between the girl and her husband is handled very well. Did you base it on people you knew?"

Gillian's heart sank. She was conscious of Trevor watching her. Another moment and he would want to know what the passages were about. She had to avoid that at all costs.

"Not really," she replied. "At least, I suppose part of it—on things I'd heard." It was unfair that joy could change to misery so soon, she thought.

Slowly the atmosphere in the room returned to something like normality. Boston said little

50

and was pointedly ignored by the others. Carole still looked upset and hardly spoke. Gillian knew Trevor was still furious and, aware how devastating his temper could be when he lost it, she was apprehensive. What on earth had possessed her to cause that scene just now? She should have moved her leg away and ignored Boston. Instead she had given way to a gleeful revenge—and she was glad. He was the sort of bumptious, common little man with an inflated sense of his own importance who needed showing up and humiliating. In the Wheatsheaf before lunch he had persisted in talking about his "Roller," as if nobody else they knew owned a Rolls. He was detestable, and if it hadn't been for Trevor, she would have had no regrets. She suspected the others were secretly applauding her.

Except Carole. Gillian was rather sorry for her, tied to a husband like the comedian. But it was her own fault; she was his fourth wife, she should have known. And he was at least thirty years older; what could she have seen in him except his money and the glamour of being the wife of a star? Well, whatever her reasons, it was plain she hated him now.

"More wine, Carole?" Chester asked. Boston,

he told himself, had had more than enough already, but let the others drink a bit more and they might begin to relax.

4

AS soon as lunch was over the party showed signs of disintegrating. To Susan it seemed as if they had been held together by some outside force and now, freed, they couldn't wait to escape from each other's company. Yet for the moment something still held them back.

Elsie, coming in to clear the table, found them still sitting round it. They watched in silence as she collected as much of the dirty crockery as she could carry and went out again.

"I've got to give a man a bell," Boston announced. "Is it all right if I use your phone, Logan, or would you rather I went and found a box? It's only a local call, I promise."

"Of course you can use it," Chester told him, irritated by this further evidence of his guest's misplaced sense of humour. "I should go in the study."

"You've got an extension?"

"Two, one in the drawing-room and one in my bedroom."

53

Boston grunted.

"Are you afraid one of us might eavesdrop on you?" Hastings asked lightly.

"I wouldn't put that past some of you," the comedian retorted.

He might have intended it as a joke, although it hadn't sounded like one, but Trevor faced him angrily. "I've had enough of you, you bloody crook," he nearly shouted. "If you don't watch it, you'll get something you haven't bargained for."

"Don't take any notice of him, Trevor," Gillian pleaded.

For a moment her husband ignored her, then he said curtly, "Come outside. I want to talk to you."

Gillian had been dreading this moment, and she was about to protest that she wouldn't go, but Trevor took her arm and half coaxed, half pushed her out of the room. They left behind them an awkward silence, broken when Chester said, "You'd better go and make your call if you're going to, Tommy."

Looking churlish, Boston stood up and went out by the other door.

"I've got to get some things at the post office," Susan said. "And I promised Miss

Rider I'd drop that book you promised in. If I take it now, she'll have it to read tomorrow." She must get away, she told herself. The very atmosphere in this room seemed malevolent. And it was all that unspeakable man's fault.

She went out the same way Boston had done, and after a moment's hesitation Carole followed her.

"That was quite the most unpleasant lunch I have ever had," Alethea remarked when they had gone. "I must say, you've excelled yourself, Logan."

For once Chester looked abashed. "How was I to know he'd behave like that?" he asked defensively. "Or Gill for that matter."

"You knew him. I should have thought that would have been enough."

"You can't take any notice of what Tommy says when he's like that."

"If you mean when he's drunk, it's hard to tell when he is and when he's sober," Alethea commented. "He behaves much the same. Such a silly man—apart from being utterly repulsive. He doesn't seem to see the danger he runs."

"Danger?" Chester was startled. "Alcoholism, you mean?"

"Oh, not that sort of danger. Didn't you see

55

the way your friend Lane was looking at him?"
Alethea stood up. "I am going to do some more reading."

"Watch out for wild beasts if you go in the garden," Chester warned her, his good humour restored.

Alethea gave him a chilly look and went out, meeting Elsie in the doorway.

"I'm going now, sir, if that's all right," Elsie told Chester. "I've left as much as I can ready. Miss Wareham knows."

"Fine, Miss Hemmings," Chester said. "Thank you very much indeed for coming today."

"That's all right, sir." Elsie departed.

"Coming outside, Peter?" Chester asked Hastings.

"Soon. I must have left my pipe in the pub; I've just got time to fetch it before closing-time. I'll see you in a few minutes."

"I'll be in the garden," Chester said.

He went out by the other door to the drawing-room and Hastings to the hall. The shortest route to the Wheatsheaf was by the side door facing him.

Chester, emerging through the French windows, saw Gillian and Trevor some distance off at the bottom of the lawn. From their attitudes he supposed they were arguing and, having no wish to involve himself in their problems, he turned and walked in the direction of the vegetable garden. Old Ben Archer who came in two days a week to do most of the gardening had said something yesterday about blackfly on the runner beans.

"What was all that about your book?" Trevor demanded.

"All what?" Gillian countered.

"You know very well what."

"I don't."

"Everybody seems to have read it except me."

"The only people who have are Logan and Alethea. I showed it to him because he was the only person I knew who could tell me if it was any good, and he asked if he could send it to her because she's his publisher and he thought it was worth trying. I told you all that, only you weren't interested. You've never been interested in what I write."

Trevor brushed the accusation aside. "What about Boston?"

"I don't know. I wouldn't have thought Logan would—"

"You and Logan! He fancies you. And you fancy him, don't you?"

"No!" Gillian retorted a little too vehemently.

"It sticks out a mile."

"I don't. I don't even know if I like him very much."

This is like a scene in a bad television play, Gillian thought. Perhaps when married people were reduced to this sort of confrontation they always talked this way. If so, the dialogue she had always so despised was accurate. But Trevor was so sure he was right. Just as he always was about everything. Why couldn't he have doubts too?

"What's it about?" he demanded.

"What's what about?" She was genuinely puzzled because she had been following her own thoughts.

"Your book."

"People. Why are you suddenly interested in it? It's taken me nearly a year to write and you've never asked me anything about it before. Now, just because that foul little man gets stoned and talks about it, you think you ought to find out something."

"That's not why," Trevor said.

"Then what is?"

"It seems as if you're keeping something a secret from me. Everybody else knows. You're cutting me out."

"And whose fault would it be if I was?" Gillian wanted to know.

"I don't care whose fault it is," Trevor said.

All right, Gillian thought, anger overcoming discretion, you want to know and I'll tell you. "It's about a young woman who marries a man who isn't as intelligent or well educated as she is because she's attracted to him physically," she said. "Only for her the attraction doesn't last. They say it never does, don't they? And all he cares about as far as she's concerned is having her available when he feels like sex and her having his children. It doesn't matter what she wants or feels about things; to him she isn't a person with a mind and feelings of her own at all, she's an appendage expected to go along with whatever he wants. It's about how they see themselves and each other, and how their families and friends see them."

Gillian stopped, appalled. Oh God! she thought. What made me do it? She was scared, not of Trevor but of what she had done to them both. Yet at the same time she was conscious

59

of a strange sense of relief, as though subconsciously she had always wanted him to know. But now he did, what would he do?

"The Wightman woman wanted to know if you'd based it on people you knew," he said quietly. "She guessed. And Boston said authors put a lot of themselves into their first books. He knew it was about us."

"But it isn't," Gillian pleaded. "There may be a little of us in it, but that's all. And he can't have known; everybody says that about first novels."

"He'd read it," Trevor insisted. "Your precious Logan must have lent it to him. You knew what would happen when you wrote it. That people would point at me and say, 'Look at him, he's the ignorant oaf in his wife's book.' You knew, but it didn't stop you. You didn't care. Or is it what you wanted to happen?"

"No," Gillian said desperately. Her heels had sunk into the turf so that she had to look up more than usual at Trevor. Nevertheless wasn't what he said partly true? The book had been born out of her frustration; hadn't she been hitting back at him when she wrote it? Just as she had contemplated an affair with Logan to revenge herself on Trevor? Why was it that now the idea was repugnant to her?

"That's why Boston thought you were easy," Trevor told her in a disgusted tone. "He thought you were ready for anything."

"No!" Gillian cried.

Trevor had gone white with anger and suddenly, without saying anything more, he turned and started striding away towards the house.

"Trevor!" Gillian called.

Chester heard her in the vegetable garden and decided to mind his own business. Ben Archer had been right about the blackfly; they'd have to spray them with something unpleasant, he supposed.

Trevor heard her, too, and took no notice.

A table and some chairs were set out on the lawn half-way to the house. Miserably Gillian walked over and sat down on one of the chairs, her shoulders drooping. What had she done? More urgently, what was Trevor going to do? She felt forlorn in a way she hadn't since she was a child.

She had been there only a minute or two when Peter Hastings came round the corner of the house. Seeing her, he walked over and sat down on another chair. His pipe was in his hand and, taking his pouch from his pocket, he began stuffing tobacco into the bowl.

"I was lucky," he remarked, "it was still on the window sill."

"I'm sorry?" Gillian dragged her thoughts back from Trevor and her own problems. There was something reassuringly calm and ordinary about Peter, she thought. He reminded her of Richard Todd as a naval officer in those old films about the war they kept showing on television, neat and reliable. Rather shy, too; he kept to himself and didn't enter into the social life of the district.

"My pipe," he explained, gesturing with it. "I left it in the Wheatsheaf before lunch."

"Oh good."

"I'm sorry. Do you mind if I smoke?"

"No, of course not."

Hastings put the pouch away, struck a match and held it to the bowl. Gillian's father hadn't smoked and Trevor smoked only an occasional thin cigar; she watched, interested and oddly soothed, as he tamped the tobacco down with his forefinger until the pipe was drawing to his satisfaction.

"What do you do?" she asked.

He regarded her, eyes half closed, through a cloud of pale-blue smoke. "I write."

"Oh." Gillian felt slightly foolish. What must he have thought during the talk about her book at lunch? she wondered. "I'm sorry, I didn't know."

"Not many people do. They ask if you write under your own name, and you know what they really mean is that they've never heard of you." Hastings smiled. "It's very depressing. As you'll discover."

"Unless you're someone like Tommy Boston," Gillian said.

He drew on his pipe and blew out smoke. "Who wants to be like him?"

It was the first time Gillian had laughed for hours.

"Where's Trevor?" Hastings asked.

"He went indoors." Had he really gone to have it out with Tommy Boston? If so, in his present mood there was no telling what he might say or do.

Out of the corner of her eye Gillian saw Chester going back into the house by the kitchen door and breathed a little sigh of relief. If Trevor and Boston were having a row, Logan would calm them down and see everything was all right. She told herself the sooner she and Trevor left the better. She had started out this morning with such high hopes, and apart from the news about her book the day had been an almost unmitigated disaster. Even the probability of the book's being published no longer seemed as important as it had.

Alethea Wightman had suggested there were things in it she would like to discuss; if she could find Alethea perhaps she could tell her she wanted to alter parts of it. But she hadn't seen Alethea since lunch.

Peter Hastings was saying something and she put thoughts of her book and Trevor out of her mind.

"I'm sorry?" she said.

"It was nothing. Just that Logan's got a lovely place here."

"Yes, he has."

Carole had come out by the French windows. Seeing them, she walked over. It occurred to Gillian she looked more composed than she had done the last time she saw her.

"Where were you, Peter?" she asked. "I looked for you just now, but I couldn't find you."

"Here," Hastings replied. "Before that I was

at the pub. I left my pipe there before lunch and I went to fetch it. Where have you been?"

"Upstairs." Carole sat down, folding her long legs under her chair. "I'd had about as much as I could stand."

"Did you see Trevor anywhere when you came down?" Gillian asked.

"No. Why? Have you lost him?"

"He went indoors."

"I didn't see him."

He couldn't have gone home without her, could he? Gillian thought. No, he wouldn't be so childish. It was far more likely he had gone to tell Boston what he thought of him and his behaviour, making his point forcibly and working the hate out of himself that way. During the eight years of their marriage she had seen Trevor twice when the laughter in his eyes had changed to cold, bitter anger, and she wasn't likely to forget the sight.

"Has Tommy really read my book?" she asked Carole.

"Don't ask me," the blond girl answered. Contempt in her voice, she added, "I shouldn't think it's very likely, he doesn't read much except things about him. Anyway, it isn't published yet, is it? How could he have read it?"

"Then why did he pretend he had?"

Carole shrugged indifferently. She didn't like Gillian much; she gave herself airs and she had started all that fuss at lunch. Just because Tommy tried to play footsie with her under the table. Not that he hadn't asked for it, pathetic old goat. Oh hell! she thought miserably.

"If you ask me, he hated being left out," Hastings said. "He had to make it look as if he knew what you and Alethea Wightman and Logan were talking about."

Gillian wondered if that was true. If it was, and Boston knew nothing about her book, the argument she had had with Trevor need never have happened. It was only Boston's pretence that he had read it, and his remarks about her having put a lot of herself into it, that had enraged Trevor. And sent him storming off to the house like that.

They talked in a desultory sort of way for a little longer, then Chester came out by the kitchen door carrying a tray of drinks. Susan was with him.

"It's only fruit cup," he said, putting the tray

down on the table. "Harmless and refreshing. Where are the others?"

"Trevor went indoors," Gillian told him.

"Tommy's there somewhere," Carole added.

"And Alethea said she was going to do some reading. I thought she was going to bring it out here. That's everybody accounted for then."

Logan was breathing hard, Gillian thought. It was hardly surprising, he must be at least two stones overweight. If he didn't look out he'd have a coronary or a stroke or something. His colour was pretty high.

He and Susan sat down on two of the vacant chairs and ten minutes passed while the five of them sipped their drinks and talked. Susan was next to Peter Hastings. Except for exchanging Good-mornings when they met in the street or at the post office, she had never spoken to him until today and it was a relief after all the tensions at lunch to chat without any demands on her nerves or emotions.

"You don't live in the village, do you?" he said.

Susan shook her head. "No, I have a flat in Breckley. Do you know it?"

"Not very well."

"It's rather a nice little village. The flat's in

an old house in Fore Street, almost opposite the church. I used to share it with another girl, but she got married and left and now I've got it to myself. It suits me. My landlady has the ground floor and I have the first. She's very nice, but we keep ourselves to ourselves and we don't see each other very often. She's away this weekend."

"You make yourself sound very self-sufficient," Hastings said with a smile.

"Do I? Perhaps I am a bit." Susan laughed and glanced across at Logan Chester, who was talking to Carole. "Not too much, though. Have you always been a writer?"

"That depends on what you mean by a writer. I was a journalist for a long time."

They chatted on, relaxed and at ease with each other.

We are all making an effort, Gillian told herself. Even Logan. But although Chester was trying to be his normal extrovert self, it was clear his heart wasn't in it. He seemed unusually subdued. And she and Carole weren't helping much, Gillian thought. Yet it was lovely here in the garden with a blackbird singing its heart out from the top of a tree in the orchard, sparrows squeaking on the lawn only a few yards from their chairs and roses, sweet peas, lupins and phlox making a riot of colour in the flower-beds. A warm, beautiful summer after-noon with the sun gently toasting her back and shoulders. So why was she—why were they all —so preoccupied? On edge, even. It was ridicu-lous that two or three crass remarks from a silly, vulgar little man could have such an effect on them. Another two or three hours and she and Trevor could leave, putting the Bostons out of their lives for ever.

She and Trevor. Thinking about him revived all her fears. He had been deeply hurt. Perhaps he saw it was partly his own fault—he had never been blind to his own shortcomings—but that was unlikely to help. Could they get back to how they had been before today? How ironic, Gillian thought, that she had written the book because she was dissatisfied with her life, and now all she wanted was to return to it.

"Tommy can't *still* be on the phone," Carole said suddenly. "It's ages."

Chester started to say something, then stopped.

"For heaven's sake let him stay in there if he wants to," Hastings said.

But Carole was already starting across the

69

lawn towards the house. Mildly irritated, because they all shared Hastings' feelings, the others watched her go in by the French windows.

"Oh dear," Chester murmured ironically.

Gillian suspected that his mood had changed and now he was secretly enjoying the situation. He seemed buoyed up and alert.

"You love stirring things, Logan, don't you?" she accused him.

"Me?" Chester's expression was all innocence.

"Yes, you. Did you show my book to Tommy Boston?"

He looked genuinely surprised. "No, of course not. He made all that up. You didn't really think he'd seen it, did you?"

"I didn't know," Gillian muttered.

"I'm hurt you should think I'd show it to anybody without asking you first," Chester told her. "Especially him. You know I asked you before I sent it to Alethea. Aren't you just the slightest bit grateful?"

Gillian felt herself flushing. "You know I am," she answered. "It was just that he seemed to know so much about it."

"A dangerous man, our favourite comedian," Chester commented.

"Is he?"

"What? Dangerous? Or our favourite comedian?"

"Both," Gillian said, smiling despite herself at Chester's expression.

"God forbid he's our favourite comedian, although I suppose thousands of people must like him. As for being dangerous—well, you've seen and heard him." In a different tone Chester went on, "Does any of what he said matter? Alethea wants to publish your book, that's all you should be thinking about. And she'll treat you fairly. Whatever her faults, she's honest."

"Why did Logan ask Boston?" Hastings murmured to Susan. "It was a crazy thing to do. I knew there'd be trouble as soon as I heard he was coming."

"I don't know," Susan answered quietly. Logan was talking to Gillian Lane and couldn't hear them. "It hasn't turned out very well, has it?" Peter was right, she reflected, people like Tommy Boston generated trouble wherever they went. Looking up, she saw Carole returning.

"He's still in there," the blond girl said. She was frowning and she sounded uncertain. "He's locked the door."

"Locked it?" Chester said. "Why should he do that?"

They all looked at each other, suddenly apprehensive.

"I'll fetch him," Chester told Carole, standing up and starting towards the French windows.

Just before he reached them Trevor came out. He was slightly flushed and Chester could smell the whisky on his breath.

"Where have you been?" he demanded.

"The pub. Why?"

"Gill's been anxious. If you must have rows, I wish you wouldn't have them here."

"Look—" Trevor began aggressively.

"All right, forget it. Boston's locked himself in the study and Carole's worried. I'm going to fetch him out." Chester strode into the drawing-room and across it to the door.

"What's he done that for?" Trevor wanted to know, following him.

"How the hell do I know?" They were in the hall now with the study door on the left. It was closed and Chester turned the knob and shook it. "Tommy!" he called. "Tommy, open the door."

They waited, but there was no answer.

"Perhaps he's not in there," Trevor suggested.

"We'll soon see."

Chester pulled open the door at the end of the hall and Trevor followed him out of the house. The study had two windows, one at the front, the other on the side only five or six feet from the door. Going up to it, they peered in.

"Oh my God!" Chester breathed.

5

TOMMY BOSTON was lying on his left side near the desk. At that time of day the sun shone on the other side of the house, leaving the study in shadow, so they could see no more. Also his face was turned away and half hidden from them.

"He must have had a heart attack," Chester said. He was aware of Hastings joining them but he didn't look round. "We've got to get in."

"Is there another key?" Trevor asked.

"I don't know. I suppose there is somewhere, but goodness knows where. We'll have to break the window."

The other men's silence might have signified consent, or merely that it was Chester's window and, therefore, his decision.

"Will you ring the doctor, Peter?" Chester said. "There's a phone in the drawing-room."

"Yes. Yes, of course." Hastings looked badly shocked, but he pulled himself together and hurried back into the house.

Chester was looking round for something with which to break the glass. While he did so Trevor examined the window to satisfy himself it was really fastened and couldn't be opened. But it was fitted with double glazing and both sections were firmly secured. So were both parts of the other window. He returned to Chester.

The flower-bed bordering the path was edged with bricks set at an angle in the soil and Chester was prising one of them loose.

"I've always wanted to do this," he remarked, straightening up with it in his hand and eyeing the window.

Trevor looked at his companion's unprotected hand and arm. "I'd throw it," he advised him.

Chester obeyed, hurling the brick so hard it shattered both panes and left wickedly jagged fragments in the frame. Pulling up another brick, he used it as a hammer to knock them out before reaching in and unfastening the catches.

The sill was waist-high and he eyed it thoughtfully.

"I'll go," Trevor volunteered, taking a step forward.

"It's all right. I will." Chester brushed the

offer aside. It seemed he wanted to show Gillian's husband he was fit and athletic enough. "You go round and I'll open the door."

It took him several seconds to heave his bulky frame up onto the sill and manoeuvre himself through the narrow space. Trevor watched until he was safely in and walking across the room to the door, then he returned to the hall. He could hear Hastings on the phone in the drawing-room. A second later a key grated in the lock and Chester opened the study door.

"Is he—?" Trevor asked. It must have been some chemical reaction, the adrenalin flowing faster or something, countering the alcohol, he no longer felt flushed and a little light-headed.

"I don't know, I haven't looked at him yet." Chester turned and squatted beside Boston. "Oh God!" he breathed.

"What is it?" Trevor bent over too. "Oh no!" His voice was as shocked as Chester's had been.

Boston was lying with his knees drawn up a little. Protruding from the back of his pale blue jacket just inside his left shoulderblade was the slim handle of a knife. The edges of the small slit the blade had cut in the cloth were caked with nearly dry blood, and there was an ominous dark pool on the carpet.

"We'll have to call the police," Trevor said.

"Yes, of course." Chester straightened up. "And we shouldn't touch anything in here. Will you tell the others while I call them?"

Trevor nodded. Tell Carole, he thought. How did you tell a woman her husband was lying dead with a knife in his back and she was a widow? Maybe theirs hadn't been the happiest or the most successful of marriages; it would still be an appalling shock. Then there would be the police with all their questions. Suspicion. He supposed none of them would escape that.

Wiping a hand across his forehead, he was surprised that when he took it away it was damp with perspiration, because inside he was quite cold.

Chester followed him out to the hall, pulling the door to behind them by holding the edge through his handkerchief well away from the knob. No doubt the police would check that for fingerprints. And they would want to know how a man had been stabbed to death in a room where the only door was locked on the inside and both windows were securely fastened. Apparently that hadn't struck Lane yet, he thought, as Trevor crossed the drawing-room and went out through the French windows.

Peter Hastings was still on the telephone. "He's not there," he said as Chester came in. "His wife, I suppose it was, gave me the number of another doctor, but I can't get any answer."

"It's too late," Chester told him. "He's dead."

"Dead?" Hastings still looked shocked and he seemed unable to take in what Chester had told him. "But he—"

"It wasn't a coronary. Somebody stabbed him with a knife."

Chester was surprised how calm he felt. Almost detached, as if he were an observer with no connection with what had happened and no involvement with anybody else here. Yet they were his guests, he thought. In a sense, his friends, although he had disliked Boston intensely.

"You mean he was . . . ?" Hastings seemed incapable of completing the question.

"Yes. People don't stab themselves in the back," Chester said, taking the telephone. "I'm going to ring the police."

"Yes, of course. You'll have to."

"Trevor's telling the others."

Chester started dialling 999, and as Hastings

went out of the room he heard him say, "Police, please."

What was happening? He couldn't believe it.

The other members of the party were sitting in a stunned group and he joined them. Carole, he saw, was very pale. She looked up as he passed and he was startled by the dead, uncomprehending expression in her eyes.

Alethea alone wasn't there.

Detective Superintendent Neil Lambert was forty-two and a well-built six feet, not yet noticeably putting on weight, nor losing any of his reddish brown hair. He had a small moustache and had once been described by a colleague with more imagination than most as looking rather like a friendly fox, probably because of his slightly pointed chin and noticeably bright eyes. His rank went with his post as head of the Divisional CID.

"Looks like an ordinary kitchen knife, sir," the scene-of-crime officer reported.

Lambert watched while he finished his work and the photographer took over, to be followed in his turn by the police surgeon. Why did he have to land a case like this for his first real murder enquiry on his own? You couldn't count that business at the fairground last autumn, a common or garden brawl which had got out of hand. Lambert had no doubt this was murder —and murder, moreover, carefully planned and executed. People didn't stab themselves in the back, nor fall with such deadly accuracy on knives wedged upright on the floor by accident. And this body had been found in a room which was to all intents and purposes sealed from the inside.

It looked like being a real pig of a case, he thought. Not some crazy yob blasting another with a shotgun, or a husband strangling his unfaithful wife; it was more like the plots of the books he wrote in his spare time under another name. The difference was they were fiction and this was real.

"I'm going to ask you how long he's been dead, and you're going to tell me you can't say, and what do I expect. Right, Doctor?" he said.

"That's right," the doctor, a small man several years older than Lambert, agreed cheerfully. "If you want me to guess, I'd say about an hour and a half, give or take twenty minutes either way. The pathologist will be able to give you a better idea after the p.m."

Lambert nodded. "You know who he is?" he asked.

"Should I?" The doctor stood up. "He looks familiar, but I can't remember where I've seen him before."

"Tommy Boston, the comedian."

"Good Lord." Dr. Felstead gave the dead man another, less professionally interested look. "I've only seen him once or twice. I suppose it would be improper to say he had it coming to him."

"Probably," Lambert agreed. Partly from inclination, partly because he hadn't the time, he rarely watched television comedy programmes. However it seemed unlikely Boston had been stabbed by an outraged viewer who couldn't stand his performances.

"It was a very tidy job, anyway," Felstead commented. "It looks as if he was stabbed through the aorta; he must have died almost at once."

"Would it have taken any medical knowledge?" Lambert asked.

"Not necessarily. It could have been chance." The doctor picked up his bag. "Oh well, I'll leave you to it. The best of luck." With a friendly nod he departed.

The body was removed on a stretcher and the fingerprint expert, a retired policeman, started work. Lambert looked round the room, absorbing the background. All he knew so far was what the uniformed sergeant, who with a constable had been the first on the scene, had reported. The house belonged to Logan Chester, the man who had the television programme, and Boston and his wife were his guests for the weekend. After lunch Boston had come to the study to make a phone call. When he hadn't reappeared after some time his wife had come to look for him. She had found the door locked and he didn't answer when she called. Chester, with a Mr. Lane, another guest, had been unable to get any reply either, so they had gone round to the window, looked in and seen Boston lying on the floor, apparently unconscious. Assuming he was ill, they had broken a window and Mr. Chester had climbed in, unlocking the door to admit Mr. Lane. It was then they discovered that Mr. Boston had been stabbed and called the police.

The brick Chester had used to smash the glass was lying amidst the shattered splinters on the carpet under the window, Lambert saw.

Now Chester and his guests were gathered in the garden, no doubt shocked and incredulous, and probably apprehensive too, waiting to be questioned. Lambert had sent WPC Graham out there with one of the uniformed constables. Other uniformed men were already making door-to-door enquiries at the houses along the road on both sides of Forge Cottage in case any of the neighbours had seen anybody near the house this afternoon. Lambert considered that if they had it was highly unlikely the person had anything to do with the murder. Everything indicated that was committed by one of the people waiting on the lawn. An outsider could only have known Boston would be in the study just then if he or she had made an appointment to meet him there. Which seemed very improbable. And there was nothing to suggest the murderer was a housebreaker Boston had surprised at work.

Everything Lambert had seen of the house spoke of money. Not ostentatious wealth, but at least comparative affluence. That mahogany desk, for instance, and the carpet, they must have cost a tidy sum. No doubt Logan Chester was comfortably off.

The fingerprint expert had finished with the side window. Chester had left it unlatched after he climbed in, and taking care to avoid the broken glass on the floor Lambert closed it and tested the catches. Both of them worked firmly and positively. So did those on the other window. It would have been impossible for the murderer to leave that way, fastening both parts behind him. So how had he gone? There was only the one door and no other way out. Not even a fireplace or a trapdoor in the ceiling.

Detective Sergeant Beeley, a sandy-haired young man with the build of a rugby forward, was examining the books on the nearest shelves. "They're all thrillers," he said in a surprised tone.

"Chester's an expert," Lambert told him. "He's written a book about them."

Beeley looked disgusted.

Lambert joined him and saw that the shelves were lined with books by authors from Wilkie Collins to P. D. James, mostly British and American, but with a few translations from other languages. There were hundreds of them, in hardback and paperback editions, together with books on the history of crime fiction and a row of reference books.

"You should have something in common, sir," Beeley ventured. Lambert's writing was an open secret in the county force.

Lambert doubted it; he remembered something Chester had once written in a review of one of his books. In any event, his writing had nothing to do with this case, and fortunately Chester wouldn't recognize his name when he heard it.

"Give me a hand with this carpet," he said.

Together they lifted first one half, then the other.

"What are we looking for?" Beeley asked.

"Trapdoors," Lambert replied.

There wasn't one. And the old dark-stained boards looked as if they had been in place as long as the house had stood.

"We'll have to take all the books down," Lambert said. "Make sure there's no secret passage out of here." He saw the sergeant's expression. "All right, I know it's a chance in a thousand, but it's an old house and we've got to look. You carry on here. I'm going to talk to the people outside."

"Right, sir." Although he didn't move, it seemed that Beeley flexed himself.

Lambert walked out to the hall, pausing on the way to examine the door and its lock. The key was in it and he turned it two or three times. It moved smoothly without any sign of wear or sloppiness. It would have been impossible, surely, for the murderer to turn it from outside. Stooping, he sniffed at the keyhole. There was no smell of oil. That might mean the murder had not been planned long in advance. On the other hand, Lambert thought wrily, it might mean nothing—except that the lock hadn't been oiled recently.

On the face of it this was an impossible crime. It wasn't, of course, Boston's dead body was proof of that, but discovering how it had been committed looked like being as difficult as finding the identity of the murderer. Straightening up, Lambert walked out to the lawn.

Chester and his guests were sitting in a silent group by the table. Perhaps the presence of WPC Graham, a pretty woman with dark curly hair, and the uniformed constable inhibited them. Not that there was anything alarming about Felicity Graham. It occurred to Lambert that she looked slimmer and less formidable in civvies than when he had seen her in uniform around the station before her attachment to CID. And definitely more attractive.

As he approached the group they looked up, and he was conscious of them watching and appraising him. One of them, a burly man whose face he recognized from seeing it in the papers and once or twice on television, stood up.

"Mr. Chester?" Lambert said. Chester might resent the implied lack of recognition, but murder enquiries had no room for personal vanities. "I'm Detective Superintendent Lambert. It's my job to make enquiries into Mr. Boston's death. I'm very sorry about the reason for my being here, but I'm sure you will understand I have to ask you all some questions. We'll take your written statements afterwards." He paused and looked at the others. "You've all been here all the afternoon?"

There was a murmur of assent.

"And, apart from Mr. Boston, nobody has been here who isn't here now?"

"No," Chester said. Then he corrected himself. "Well, Miss Hemmings, the lady from the village who does my housework, helped with our lunch. But she left after she'd cleared the table."

Lambert nodded. "Perhaps I could see you first, Mr. Chester," he said. "Is there somewhere we can go?"

"The drawing-room?" Chester suggested.

"Good." Lambert looked at the young policewoman. "Miss Graham, I shall need you to take notes."

Chester led the way across the lawn and in by the French windows to an airy room with large, comfortable furniture and several water-colours hung between the beams which criss-crossed the walls. Like Alethea Wightman, Lambert liked the room immediately, and also like her he thought that it didn't fit his image of Chester. Perhaps that image needed revising.

"Should I ask you to sit down?" Chester asked. "Anyway do."

They sat in two of the easy chairs, Chester watchful, but seeming as much at ease as could be expected in the circumstances, Lambert facing him. Felicity Graham, known to her friends and colleagues by her school nickname of Flick, seated herself on an upright chair near the window and took out her notebook and a ball-point pen.

"I understand the people on the lawn are your guests for the weekend," Lambert said. "Is that right?"

"Not exactly." Chester looked at his hands resting on the arms of his chair. "The Bostons and Miss Wightman are—were—staying, the Lanes and Peter Hastings came just before lunch. Miss Wareham's my secretary; she's here just for the afternoon too."

"So you were all here from, say, twelve o'clock?"

"Yes."

"Can you tell me when you finished lunch?"

"Not exactly. I suppose it must have been about a quarter past two."

"And afterwards you all did what?"

Chester thought for a moment. "The Lanes went out to the garden. Tommy said he had to ring somebody and could he call from here. I told him to use the phone in the study because it was more private there. Miss Wareham had to go to the post office for some things and to take a book I'd promised to lend to an old girl who lives across the green. Carole, Mrs. Boston, went upstairs, I think. After a minute or two Miss Wightman said she was going to do some reading, and Peter Hastings went to the pub to fetch his pipe. He'd left it there when we all went for a drink before lunch. I went out to the garden."

"Alone?"

"Yes. Ben Archer, who does most of the gardening, said there was blackfly coming on the runner beans and I went to have a look at them."

Leaving his guests to their own devices, Lambert reflected. He wondered if Chester had had any reason for not joining the Lanes. "That's very clear," he said.

Chester shrugged. "I have that kind of memory—and I've been thinking about it for the last hour and a half."

Lambert smiled. "I'm sure you have. Was this a purely social party, Mr. Chester? I mean, was there any business reason for it, or was business discussed at all?"

"No, it was purely social."

"And you've no idea who Mr. Boston phoned?"

"None at all. Except that he said it was a local call."

Lambert glanced across at Flick, who was writing busily. "What happened after you went out to the garden?" he asked.

"Nothing much," Chester said. "People just wandered about and talked. It wasn't the sort of party where everybody plays tennis or something. I saw Trevor Lane come into the house, and Peter Hastings come back from the pub and start talking to Mrs. Lane, and I came in to get some drinks." He smiled. "Only fruit cup. While I was in the kitchen Susan came back. Miss Wareham. She helped, and we took the drinks outside to the others. Mrs. Boston had joined them by then."

"When you were in the kitchen, did you happen to notice whether the study door was open or shut?" Lambert asked.

"It was open."

"You're sure?"

"Positive. I looked in to see if Tommy was still on the phone, but he wasn't there. Nobody was." Chester paused, but Lambert said nothing, and after a moment he went on. "After Susan and I took the drinks out we all sat talking for twenty minutes, then Carole Boston said she was coming to see where Tommy was. She was only in here a minute or two, and when she came back she said he was in the study with the door locked, and he didn't answer. I told her I'd see what he was up to and get him to come out. I was afraid he might be ill."

"Oh?" Lambert said.

"He looked like a prime candidate for a coronary or a stroke."

"Did Mrs. Boston know he was in the study?

He might have been in their bedroom, or somewhere else, mightn't he?"

"Yes. I suppose she assumed he was in the study because he had been on the phone earlier and she hadn't seen him since. I couldn't see why he should have gone back and locked the door, but he was a strange character in some ways. As I came in I met Trevor Lane and he went with me. We tried the study door and shouted, but there was no answer, so we went round to the side window and looked in. We could see Tommy lying on the floor, and we assumed he had been taken ill. Peter Hastings had come, too, by then. We came in here to call the doctor while I broke the window and climbed in, and opened the door for Trevor."

"You said Mr. Lane had come into the house earlier," Lambert observed. "Do you know where he was between then and when you met him?"

"I think he went across to the pub," Chester replied with evident reluctance.

It seemed strange to Lambert that first Hastings, then Lane should leave the party to go off to a pub by themselves. It was understandable Hastings should have gone to retrieve his pipe, but what reason had Lane had?

"Do you happen to know what the time was when you came in to get the drinks?" he asked.

"Yes, it was twenty-eight minutes to three. I looked at my watch because I wondered how much longer Miss Wareham was likely to be gone," Chester replied.

"And when you climbed in the key was in the lock on the inside of the study door?"

"Yes."

Lambert waited, but Chester said nothing more. He was watching the superintendent with a half-apologetic expression that seemed to say he understood his problem and was only sorry he couldn't help. At the same time Lambert had the impression he was still tense, even while he seemed so sure of himself. Was it only the natural tension they must all be feeling, or was he keeping something back?

"You are sure both parts of the window were securely latched?" he asked.

"Quite sure."

It was very quiet. Flick's pen was poised, ready for the next question and answer. Beyond her, Lambert could see the other members of the party seated in an uneasy group, the young policeman a few feet away. He wondered why he felt there was something false about

93

Chester's manner. Was the other man trying just a little too hard to seem frank and helpful?

"Did you notice the time when you came in to find Mr. Boston?" he asked.

"It was three minutes past three."

"And when you looked to see what was the matter with him you saw the knife. Did you recognize it?"

"No," Chester said. "I was too shocked to take much notice, and I only saw the handle. It looked like an ordinary kitchen knife."

Lambert nodded. "I wonder if you'd mind looking to see if any of your knives are missing, Mr. Chester?"

"I wouldn't mind, but it wouldn't be much use. I wouldn't know if they were all there or not. You'd do better to ask Miss Hemmings, she'd tell you straightaway."

"I'll do that," Lambert said.

They went through what Chester had told him again, then Lambert asked if he would be good enough to ask Mr. Lane to come in next.

"Yes, of course." Some of the self-assurance seemed to have gone out of Chester as he walked towards the French windows. Perhaps the reality of what had happened was only now sinking in.

94

"Just one other thing," Lambert told him casually. "What sort of man was Mr. Boston?"

It seemed almost as if Chester had been waiting for the question. "Sort of man?" he repeated.

"You knew him fairly well, I imagine."

"As a matter of fact, I hardly knew him. If you're asking what I thought of him, he was conceited, ignorant, and thoroughly unpleasant. He made a nuisance of himself with Miss Wightman this morning, and he did his best to cause a scene at lunch. I should think anybody here would cheerfully have stuck a knife in him. In theory, of course." Chester hesitated as though he was considering saying something else, but, if he was, he changed his mind, added only, "I'll tell Trevor Lane," and went out.

"Phew!" Flick exclaimed.

Lambert was looking thoughtful. "That was interesting," he remarked.

"He didn't like him much, did he, sir?"

"Not so you'd notice it, no. I wonder if the others felt the same."

Apart from Chester's opinion of the dead man, two things in particular in his account interested Lambert. One, he had been very vague about times before two-thirty, but surprisingly positive about them after that, and, two, why, if he disliked Boston so much, had he invited him here for a "purely social" weekend?

Perhaps the reason was sitting out there on the lawn: Carole Boston was an extremely attractive woman.

6

STUDYING Trevor as he came into the room Lambert thought he recognized a familiar type, a man who had built up a successful business by his own efforts, devoting most of his time and energy to it and taking other people for granted. Men like that were usually impatient, dogmatic and quick-tempered. Sometimes they were ruthless. And while all in favour of law and order in theory, they tended to regard any law which restricted them personally as fit only to be broken.

"I'm trying to get the times clear," he explained when they were sitting down and Flick had her ball-point raised. Get Lane to relax and he would probably co-operate. Unless he had killed Boston. Antagonize him and he would be as difficult as he could. "Do you know when you finished lunch?"

"Lunch?" Trevor sounded surprised. "About two, I suppose. I didn't notice."

"And then?"

"That—" Trevor had been about to use an

abusive term to describe Boston, but he stopped himself and went on: "Boston said he had to make a phone call and wanted to know if there was an extension because he wouldn't trust one of us not to listen in on it if he used the phone in the study. He was an offensive little—"

Lambert reflected that Chester hadn't mentioned Boston's saying that. In all likelihood it meant nothing. On the other hand, the call could have been confidential and Boston anxious no one should overhear it. Either way, just possibly it could have some bearing on his death. They would have to try to trace it.

"That was all he said?" he enquired casually. "He didn't mention who he had to ring or anything?"

"No, just that it was a local call."

"What did you do?"

"My wife and I went out to the garden. We'd had enough by that time."

"Do you know how long you stayed there?"

"No." Trevor saw Lambert eyeing him and added sulkily, "It must have been about ten minutes."

"And then?"

"I went across to the Wheatsheaf for a drink."

"Just like that? By yourself?"

"Yes."

Lambert saw the anger stirring in the other man. "You'd been there before lunch, hadn't you?" he asked easily.

"What about it? I went again. There's no law against it, is there?"

"Not that I know of," Lambert agreed. Youngsters drifted in and out of parties, to pubs and back, he thought, but that was different. "How long did you stay there?" he asked.

"Until they threw us out."

Trevor confirmed what Chester had said about their going to find Boston and seeing him lying on the study floor, and Chester's climbing in. When they had found that the comedian had been stabbed he had gone to break the news to the other members of the party.

"You're sure both windows were fastened?" Lambert asked him. "They couldn't have been just sticking?"

"No, I tried them while Chester was finding a brick to break the glass with. The double glazing was latched too."

"And the key was in the door."

"Yes, of course it was."

Lambert paused. "Which way did you go when you went to the pub?"

"By the side door."

"Did you notice if the study door was open or shut?"

"No, I didn't."

"And when you came back?"

"It was shut, I suppose. I wasn't taking any notice, but it must have been, mustn't it?"

"Probably," Lambert agreed. "You came back the same way then?"

"Yes," Trevor answered.

"Had you met Mr. Boston or his wife before today?"

Probably only an experienced observer would have noticed the momentary hesitation before Trevor said, "No."

"So you know of no reason why anybody should kill him?" Lambert asked.

Either Trevor didn't care or he felt too strongly about the dead man to keep his opinions to himself, Lambert wasn't sure which. In any event, he expressed them forcefully. Clearly if he had ever heard of *de mortuis*, he regarded it as effete and outmoded nonsense. "And you can make what you like of that," he concluded truculently.

Lambert was inclined to make nothing of it. After all, Logan Chester had said much the same.

For some reason, he thought when Trevor had gone, Lane was uneasy. Was it because he had something to hide? Almost certainly he had been lying when he said he hadn't seen Boston before today. On the other hand, his uneasiness might result from nothing more than an argument with his wife. About Boston? Perhaps. That would help to explain his feelings about the comedian. Lambert, who had been divorced three years before, knew only too well how women could put you in the wrong with no trouble at all. And afterwards, when you apologized for what you hadn't done, they forgave you magnanimously.

"I think we'll have Hastings in next," he told Flick.

"I'm not staying here any longer," Alethea declared. She stood up, her determination only slightly marred by her ungainly movements. She was not a graceful woman, and the flimsy garden chair didn't help.

"Don't you think we should wait?" Susan suggested.

"What for?" Alethea demanded.

"Until the superintendent has seen us all," Susan answered. She would not be intimidated. Alethea, she considered, was being ridiculous, putting on these absurdly regal airs. Didn't she understand this was a murder inquiry, and she must be one of the suspects? They all were.

"No, I don't. I've waited quite long enough already," Alethea said tartly. "If he wants to see me, he can send somebody to tell me so. Though why he should, I can't imagine. I can tell him nothing, I was in my room when that—" Out of the corner of her eye she saw Carole and stopped. "I know nothing about what happened, and I see no point in his wasting his time and mine asking me any questions."

"Bravo," Chester said ironically.

Alethea glared at him and decided to treat his flippancy with disdain. Her dislike of her host was increasing by the minute. It was his fault she found herself in this distasteful situation now; he had invited that detestable little man here.

Gillian would dearly have liked to talk to Alethea about her book, but if this was the place, it certainly wasn't the time, and she said nothing.

"He's sending for somebody now," Trevor remarked as Flick emerged through the French windows. He looked up at Alethea and added with a touch of malice, "Maybe it's your turn for the third degree."

Alethea ignored him and started walking towards the house.

"Do you think it's possible?" Chester asked in a stunned voice.

"Do we think what's possible?" Hastings wanted to know.

"That she did it," Chester said. "She's cool enough—and she hated Tommy. There's nothing to prove she was in her room all the time."

They stared at Alethea's retreating back.

It was apparent to Lambert that Hastings was tense, although the author did his best to conceal it and gave his account of what had happened quietly and concisely.

"Did you meet any other member of the party on your way to or from the pub?" Lambert asked him.

"Not one of the party exactly," Hastings

answered. "I think Elsie Hemmings was in the kitchen when I went."

He confirmed what Chester and Trevor Lane had already said about their seeing Boston through the study window, and Chester's asking him to call the doctor. He had still been trying unsuccessfully when Chester came, told him Boston had been stabbed and took over the phone to ring the police.

"I couldn't believe it," he said. "It didn't seem possible."

His disbelief appeared to be genuine, Lambert thought. "Had you met Mr. Boston before today?" he asked.

He had expected the answer to be no, but instead Hastings said, "Yes, I had."

"You knew him well?"

"Pretty well." The author hesitated. "I don't suppose it matters talking about it now he's dead. Death cancels all contracts, doesn't it? I ghosted his autobiography. It was part of the agreement I wouldn't let anybody know."

"What sort of man was he?" Lambert asked. Chester and Lane, who claimed they had hardly known the dead man, had disliked him intensely; would Hastings, who knew him better, have seen him differently?

He hesitated, as if choosing his words with care. "To use a very old-fashioned expression, he was a swine," he said. "I suppose one shouldn't say that now he's dead, but he was the most loathsome human being I've ever met. He was vain, overbearing, ignorant, loud-mouthed, uncouth, foul-minded and a pathological liar. At lunch today he pretended he'd written his damned book himself. Done all the research, everything. I asked him if he'd written many books, to see what he'd say, and he said "One or two." As if he'd written a dozen or more, but didn't want to boast about them. And he had the nerve to say his so-called autobiography was badly written. He was daring me to let the cat out of the bag, because he could go for me if I did, and he knew damned well I couldn't afford a court case. Him! He couldn't put two words together, unless they both had four letters."

Lambert wondered if Hastings realized that he was providing himself with a motive for killing Boston when nobody else seemed to have had one. Yet. But perhaps he was the sort of person who had to be frank regardless of the consequences. Certainly he had painted a clearer picture of the dead man than either Chester or Lane.

"The funny thing was, he could be quite pleasant when he wanted something," Hastings went on. "Charming. That's how he persuaded four women to marry him. It was only afterwards they found out what he was really like. I've talked to them."

Lambert waited, and when the author said nothing more, he asked, "Did you look in through the study window yourself?"

"No. I couldn't see past the other two. Anyway, there was no need, they could see he was there."

"Yes. Thank you, Mr. Hastings."

"That's all?"

"For the time being. One of my men will take a written statement from you, and it's possible we shall have to ask you some more questions later, but it's all for now."

Hastings nodded and went out.

"They all confirm each other's stories," Lambert observed to Flick when he had gone.

"Boston wasn't what you'd call popular, was he?" Flick said. "Not exactly everybody's favourite comedian."

"No," Lambert agreed. "Let's see what Mrs. Lane has to say."

Gillian looked composed. She was a beautiful woman, Lambert thought, and most likely a spoilt one. The two often went together. Lovely girls were spoilt by their parents when they were children, by too many attentive young men later, and by their husbands after they were married. By other men, too. It was in the nature of things, and he wouldn't have minded spoiling this one himself.

Her background, he suspected, was very different from her husband's.

Gillian confirmed that when they went out into the garden after lunch they had talked for about ten minutes, then he had gone off to the pub, and she had sat on the lawn where Peter Hastings had joined her a minute or two later.

"Did Mr. Lane tell you where he was going?" Lambert asked.

"Oh yes."

"But you didn't want to go with him?"

"No. I don't drink much, and I had had two martinis before lunch and a little wine with it. I didn't want any more."

On the face of it her explanation was reasonable enough, but Lambert had a feeling there was more to it than that. They would have to check with the landlord when Lane had left the Wheatsheaf; none of the party had seen him until Chester met him on his way to find Boston just after three o'clock.

"Was Mr. Lane angry about what had happened at lunch?" he asked.

Gillian became noticeably more tense. "What do you mean?" she demanded. "What happened?"

"I don't know, Mrs. Lane." Chester had said Boston tried to make a scene; Lambert was sure now it had somehow involved the woman opposite him. "Did something happen?"

Gillian knew she had been tricked, and her colour rose. She was angry with herself and with Lambert. "It was all so pathetic," she said.

"What was?"

"Mr. Boston put his hand on my leg under the table." Despite herself Gillian blushed. But it wasn't the memory of Boston's unwelcome attentions which embarrassed her, it was her own reaction to them.

"And Mr. Lane objected?" Lambert asked.

"No. I mean . . . Oh, I don't suppose he

liked it, but he thought Tommy was just trying to play footsie. We didn't talk about it."

"I'm sorry, I have to ask. What did you talk about?"

"Nothing to do with—with what's happened," Gillian said. "It was about a book I've written. Logan—Mr. Chester—sent it to Miss Wightman. She's his publisher; I suppose you know that. He invited us today so that I could meet her. She and Logan and I were talking about it at lunch. Trevor hasn't read it and he wanted to know what it was about."

And when she told him he stalked off to the pub, Lambert thought. It seemed a curious reaction. And he had gone through the house.

"Had you met Mr. Boston before?" he asked.

"No."

"Nor his wife?"

"No. We didn't know they were going to be here until we arrived; Logan hadn't told me."

He hadn't told *her*? Lambert thought. Did that explain why Trevor Lane seemed the odd one out in the party: his wife was Logan Chester's friend and he had been invited only because of her?

It seemed she could add nothing to what he already knew about the others' movements that afternoon, nor was she sure exactly when they had finished lunch. They went through her story again, then Lambert let her go.

He reflected that no one else had mentioned Boston's under-the-table activities at lunch. Chester had hinted at something, but perhaps he had been thinking of the potential row with Hastings, and nobody but Gillian and her husband knew about them. In any case, they were hardly an adequate motive for murder. While any husband might resent such behaviour, it didn't merit pistols at dawn. Nor a kitchen knife in the study.

Lambert was inclined to believe Gillian's account of her talk with Trevor in the garden, but, while true, it was probably not the whole truth. And what people didn't tell you was often more informative than what they said.

7

IT looked like being a long evening, Lambert told himself. And it was Saturday. Roger Beeley, no doubt, was already thinking about the snooker and beers with his friends he would miss. And Felicity Graham?

"Had you a date this evening?" he asked her.

The girl smiled ruefully. "Yes, sir."

"I'm afraid you won't be able to keep it. That's what working in CID does to you."

"I've had to break dates before," Flick said defensively. CID people always seemed to think they worked twice as hard as anyone else in the force.

"I'm sure you have," Lambert agreed. "Do you want to ring anybody?"

"It's all right, thank you, sir. We have an arrangement now." But how much longer would Roy stand for this sort of thing? Flick wondered.

Susan came in through the French windows and Lambert stood up. For a moment, with her back to the light, she was only a silhouette, then she moved and he saw a slim, dark young woman, not exactly pretty, but attractive nonetheless. There was character in her rather thin features, and her fine grey eyes regarded him frankly. She looked a reliable, straightforward girl. But appearances could be deceptive.

She sat down and smoothed her skirt over her knees.

"How long have you worked for Mr. Chester, Miss Wareham?" Lambert asked her.

"Eight months. Since soon after he came to live here."

"Did you know any of the guests before today?"

"Miss Wightman slightly. I'd seen Mr. Hastings and Mrs. Lane in the village, but we'd never said more than 'Good morning' or 'Nice day, isn't it?'"

"You hadn't met either of the Bostons?"

Lambert thought he detected a tiny hesitation before Susan answered, "No," but she spoke firmly enough.

"I gather Mr. Boston wasn't very popular." He paused, but she said nothing. "Do you know why Mr. Chester asked him here this weekend?"

"You had better ask him that."

"I will. I just wondered if you knew."

"No."

She might not know, but she hadn't approved, Lambert thought.

"What did you have for lunch?" he asked.

The question clearly surprised Susan, and he thought she seemed relieved at the change of subject.

"Pâté, fresh salmon and a salad, raspberries and cream, and cheese," she answered.

"And coffee afterwards?" Lambert suggested. "With brandy or liqueurs?"

"Yes. Is it important?"

"I don't know, Miss Wareham. It's a fact, that's all. We can't tell at this stage which ones will turn out to be relevant, and which won't. We just have to collect as many as possible."

They had finished lunch at ten past two, Susan said. She was sure of the time because she had looked at the clock. As soon as people started moving she had gone to the post office to buy one or two things they needed, and on to take a book to old Miss Rider. She believed Carole Boston had followed her out of the dining-room, but she couldn't swear to it, and, anyway, she didn't know where the girl had gone then.

"Which way did you leave the house?" Lambert asked.

"By the side door."

"Do you know when you got back?"

"Yes, it was twenty to three." Susan gave a half-smile. "I'm not usually so sure about times; I looked at my watch because I felt guilty about being gone so long. Mrs. Rayment at the post office likes a chat, she kept me for a little while, and Miss Rider's more or less an invalid so I didn't like to rush away. She knew Mr. Chester had visitors, and she wanted to know all about them—in the nicest possible way, of course."

There was an undertone of amusement in Susan's voice, and Lambert guessed she had a nicely ironic sense of humour. She would make a good witness, too, he thought, cool and concise.

"Did you come back into the house the same way?" he asked her.

She shook her head. "No, the door had stuck. It does sometimes. So I came round to the back. Mr. Chester was in the kitchen making some fruit cup to take out to the others, and I helped."

She could tell Lambert nothing else which added to what he already knew.

Susan was in the drawing-room with Lambert, Alethea had gone up to her room, and Chester and the Lanes, having been questioned, had wandered off. Only Carole and Hastings were left sitting on the lawn.

"I've had enough of hanging about out here," Hastings muttered.

"You don't have to wait," Carole told him. "The others have gone."

Hastings looked at her, and when she saw the expression in his eyes she gave him a tremulous little smile.

"It's different for them, isn't it?" he said.

Carole was glad he didn't want to leave her to wait for Lambert's summons alone. She should have been shattered by this afternoon's events, she supposed, and in a way she was, yet her dominating feeling was one of anticlimax. For the last year she had lived on her nerves; now, suddenly, that was over, and she felt strangely flat. And tired. Oh, so tired.

It wasn't like her, usually she was full of vitality. Or had been until recently. It was shock, she supposed, wearily pushing back the curtain of blond, perfumed hair which had fallen forward across her face.

"Let's walk about," Hastings suggested.

Carole eyed the policeman sitting a few yards away. He was young, probably younger than her, and almost as fair; he didn't look very formidable. "Should we?" she asked. "The superintendent may want me in a minute."

"He can send for you if he does. We shan't be far away."

Like Alethea, Carole thought. Had Logan been serious when he hinted she might have stabbed Tommy? One of them had—and it was true that nobody had seen her in her room all the afternoon. She could have slipped out for a few minutes without any of them knowing. Carole almost hoped it was Alethea, she didn't like her.

"All right," she agreed, standing up. She might have a trained dancer's ability to hold awkward positions, but it was a relief now just to move.

The constable started to stand up, unsure whether he should stop them. He hadn't been given orders to prevent people moving about, but Mr. Lambert hadn't questioned Mrs.

Boston yet, and if she wasn't here when he wanted her, he could be in trouble.

"It's all right, we're only going to the end of the lawn to stretch our legs," Hastings told him.

The constable sat down again, reassured. They couldn't leave the garden that way.

Carole and Hastings strolled slowly across the close-cropped turf to the bottom of the lawn where the trees and shrubs started. They were very near the spot where Boston had found Alethea that morning. Carole hesitated and looked back over her shoulder at the policeman, but he was taking no notice of them, and Hastings put an arm round her waist, urging her on.

"Oh, Peter," she sighed. For a moment she didn't speak, then she asked, as if she couldn't put it out of her mind for more than a minute or two at a time, "What did the superintendent ask you?"

"Just routine stuff," Hastings told her. "What we did this afternoon, what time we finished lunch, whether I knew you and Tommy before today. There's nothing for you to worry about. He seems quite human, and he's bound to treat you gently."

"I can't believe all this is happening," Carole said.

"Neither can I."

"Who can have done it, Peter? Have you any idea?"

"No."

"If the police knew about us . . ."

"How can they know?" Hastings sounded unconcerned. "Anyway, what difference would it make?" He put his other arm round Carole and kissed her.

After a moment's hesitation, she responded. People were wrong about Peter, she thought. They thought he was dull, but he wasn't. She had thought so too at first, when he came to see Tommy about that silly book; then, as she came to know him better, she saw he could be fun when he tried. And when she'd needed somebody because of how Tommy behaved, he was always there for her to turn to. He wasn't even shy, he just couldn't be bothered to be interesting when he was with people he didn't care about. He was one of those people who were at their worst in parties; he simply dropped out.

"We ought to get back," she said, moving a little away from him. "We don't want the

118

superintendent sending somebody to look for me."

"All right," Hastings agreed.

They turned and started walking back.

Alethea was in her room when Flick came to find her, and she agreed to accompany her to the drawing-room with an air of majestic disapproval Flick would have found laughable if it hadn't been so irritating.

To Lambert, Alethea's manner was vague in the extreme. She seemed hardly to understand what had happened or the importance of his questions and the answers she gave. Lambert had heard authors on her list swear her vagueness was a cloak for a very shrewd, tough personality, and he suspected she was exaggerating it now to avoid giving direct answers. That might indicate uncertainty or, possibly, guilt.

She said that after lunch she had stayed in the dining room for a minute or two talking to Logan Chester and Hastings. Then she had gone up to her room to continue the reading she had started in the garden that morning.

"A new novel," she explained airily. "No

good, of course. Very few of them are. *So* depressing."

Lambert suppressed a smile. "Not Mrs. Lane's book?" he asked.

"Oh no. No, that's really quite good."

"What is it about, Miss Wightman?"

Alethea's eyes opened wide. "A young woman and her husband. Their relationship, and their relationships with other people. Yes, it's very well done."

"Her relationships with other men?" Lambert suggested.

"Other men and women. People are men and women, Superintendent." Almost spitefully, Alethea added, "I don't think it would be your kind of book."

Lambert let that pass. She was probably right. "How long did you stay in your room?" he asked.

"I've no idea."

"You know when you came down?"

"Oh, when Logan Chester came to tell me that dreadful man was dead. I've no idea what the time was."

"And until then you hadn't left your room since you went up after lunch?" Lambert persisted.

"No, I'm sure I hadn't."

Did Alethea Wightman realize that she, almost alone of the party, had no alibi for the time when Boston must have been killed? Lambert wondered. If she did, she seemed blandly indifferent to the implications. Perhaps she simply couldn't conceive that she might be suspected.

"Did you see or hear anything while you were up there?" he asked.

"No. I'm sorry I can't be more helpful, Superintendent, but when I'm working I become totally immersed in what I'm doing. Totally," Alethea added with a hint of self-satisfaction.

Lambert banished the picture which sprang to his mind of her being baptized like that and asked, "What happened between you and Mr. Boston this morning?"

Alethea's eyes met his, and there was no vagueness in them now. Rather, there was loathing. "I do not wish to discuss it," she said coldly.

"I'm sorry, I must ask you to tell me," Lambert insisted.

There was an appreciable silence before Alethea said resentfully, "Very well, if you must know. I was sitting in a deck-chair reading a script. He came and pretended to help me up. But he deliberately pulled too hard, so that I was off balance, and when I stumbled he grasped me and kissed my neck. That revolting man! He practically slobbered, it was disgusting. I bit his ear hard. It was all I could do, and I was delighted to see it bled. Quite a lot. That was all."

The mind boggles, Lambert thought. The idea of the lecherous comedian, whose four wives had all been glamorous girls in their early twenties, and who had apparently fancied his chances with the lovely Gillian Lane, being seized with a sudden uncontrollable urge to embrace Alethea Wightman was so ludicrous he found it difficult to keep a straight face. Behind him Flick coughed suddenly.

Yet it must be true, Lambert told himself. It was inconceivable Alethea would invent a story which made her look slightly ridiculous, however much the innocent victim she had been.

"You didn't like him then?" he said.

"I disliked him intensely."

"Your firm published his autobiography; had you met him before?"

"Yes." Alethea's mouth clamped shut.

Lambert decided not to pursue that line. After all, she had admitted she disliked Boston. It occurred to him that the comedian's violent death might well result in a revival of the book's sales—but if Alethea had killed him to achieve that, it was the most bizarre motive for murder he had heard in a long time.

He asked her a few more questions, then told her he needn't trouble her any longer for the present. She departed in an aura of lofty indignation.

"Crikey!" Flick said when the door had shut behind her.

Lambert grinned. "Don't underestimate her," he said. "She's no fool, whatever she may seem."

"When do you think we'll be able to go?" Gillian asked Trevor. She had suggested rather tentatively they come out here to the garden, and been pleased as well as a little surprised when he agreed. The heat of the afternoon had mellowed as the shadows lengthened across the lawn, and in other circumstances she would have enjoyed being here. Now it was all spoilt and she was afraid.

"Goodness knows," Trevor replied. "When

you've given your statement, I suppose." He had already given his, taken down in laborious longhand by a uniformed constable.

"They might let you go," Gillian said, hoping he would decline the implied offer.

And he did. "I'm not leaving you here," he told her gruffly. Gillian was more pleased than she had expected. "I just want to get home," she said. She would feel safer there, even though she knew it was an illusion, and the danger she felt was threatening them could reach out to them there as well as here. It was a primitive urge to go to ground, to lose oneself in familiar surroundings.

"I've been wanting to go ever since we got here," Trevor said in a flat tone.

Gillian wasn't going to argue about that now. She wanted desperately to heal the breach between them, and she was both delighted and relieved that Trevor seemed to want the same thing. Even to her her motives weren't very clear. Partly there was a feeling that they must face the half-perceived danger together or go under, partly the knowledge that she had nearly destroyed their marriage. At the time it had hardly seemed to matter, but she realized when she saw Trevor striding away across the lawn this afternoon, his face tight with anger, that the life she had was the one she really wanted. That she should have seriously considered endangering it by her book and an affair with Logan appalled her.

She no longer felt attracted to Logan. He had been kind and helpful, reading her book and sending it to Alethea Wightman, but that was 'as far as it went. It was hard to believe she had ever been drawn to the man he claimed to be. Her pride rebelled at the notion of being just one more in the succession of women he had had as his mistresses.

Why had he asked the Bostons this weekend? Was he having an affair with Carole?

Gillian's thoughts went off at a tangent and she screwed up her courage to ask one of the questions which had been troubling her ever since Peter Hastings came out and told them what had happened. "Trevor," she said diffidently, "where did you really go this afternoon?"

He looked at her, an expression she couldn't read in his eyes. "I told you, the pub."

"Is that the truth? You didn't go anywhere else?"

"Don't you believe me?"

He didn't know how much she wanted to,

Gillian thought. "Of course I do, if you say so," she answered. But even to her the words sounded stilted and unconvincing.

"You think I killed Boston, is that it?"

"No. No, I don't. It's just that you were gone so long." Gillian stopped, afraid to go on. "Who do you think stabbed Tommy?"

"If you really want to know," Trevor told her, "I reckon it was your friend Logan."

Gillian was startled. "Why him?"

"Well, for one thing, he invited the Bostons here."

"That doesn't make him a murderer. He can't have done it, he was with Peter and Carole and Susan and me out here."

"And I wasn't," Trevor said.

"I didn't mean that," Gillian told him, distressed. "I was thinking about Alethea. Logan was right, she says she was in her room, but she can't prove it. And she hated Tommy."

"Nobody can have done it," Trevor said. "The windows were fastened and the door was locked on the inside. He must have killed himself."

"But he was stabbed in the back. You can't commit suicide like that." Gillian shuddered.

"Do you think the superintendent will let us go when I've given my statement?"

"He can't stop us."

Gillian wasn't sure Trevor was right, and she suspected it would be unwise to put his idea to the test. She sighed.

8

CHESTER'S guests came in one after the other, said their pieces and departed. Like applicants being interviewed for a job, Flick thought as Carole came into the room. Or actors at an audition. Perhaps they were actors, each giving his own performance, none quite true.

Lambert had kept Boston's widow until last, partly to allow her longer to recover from the initial shock of his death, and partly because he wanted to hear what the others had to say before seeing her. She looked strained, but fairly composed, the dress she had worn earlier changed for a darker one which covered her shoulders. She was wearing only a little make-up, and her only jewellery was her wedding ring and a diamond solitaire on the same finger. Lambert wondered if she had removed both make-up and jewellery since this afternoon, either in deference to the circumstances or for his benefit. She accepted his condolences awkwardly, with a murmured, "Thank you," and perched on the edge of the easy chair facing him.

"You knew Mr. Chester before this weekend, I believe?" he said.

"Tommy did, I'd only seen him once—and then it was only to say hallo to at a party," Carole answered.

"Did they get on well?"

"I suppose they must have done. I mean, if they didn't, why did Logan ask us here?"

That, Lambert reflected, was one of the most intriguing questions in this whole business. Clearly by this afternoon any liking Chester might have felt for the comedian had gone, replaced by a cordial dislike. Had that happened only since the Bostons' arrival yesterday?

"As far as you know, he hadn't any special reason?" he asked. Carole shook her head. "No."

She could think of nothing that had happened or been said either last night or this morning which could have had any bearing on this afternoon's events, except, possibly, her husband's being cut. She didn't know how it happened, but he had come in swearing about "That bloody bitch." As there was no other woman about, she had assumed he meant Alethea, although it was hard to believe she had actually attacked him.

"I didn't want to know," Carole admitted.

Lambert believed her. He asked her about lunch that day, and wasn't surprised when she said nothing about her husband's behaviour; she must have found it humiliating.

"Nothing happened that seems significant now?" he asked. "Nothing unusual?"

He noticed the slight hesitation before she answered, "No, nothing. Mostly we talked about holidays and television programmes."

"Mr. Boston said he'd written some books, I believe."

"He didn't actually say he'd written them, he just sort of hinted he had."

"Was it true, Mrs. Boston?"

"I don't know. That's the truth. We'd only been married fifteen months, he may have written them before I knew him."

"But surely, if he had, he wouldn't have engaged Mr. Hastings to write his auto-biography, would he?"

"No, I don't suppose so," Carole agreed.

Clearly she had known about her husband's arrangement with Hastings, Lambert thought.

But then, the book had almost certainly been written, partly at least, since she and Boston were married.

She said she had no idea whom Tommy had phoned.

"Did you go to speak to him when you left the dining-room?" Lambert asked her.

"No. I was going to, but he'd gone into the study and shut the door. I could hear him talking on the phone, so I went upstairs to freshen up and get a magazine to read. Then I went out to the garden. Peter Hastings and Gill Lane were out there, and I sat talking to them until Logan and Susan Wareham came out with drinks."

"Did you hear what Mr. Boston was saying on the phone?"

"No, just that he was talking."

Lambert wondered if that was true, but he didn't press the point. Instead he asked, "What did you talk about on the lawn?"

"Nothing much. Gill wanted to know if I'd seen Trevor, but I hadn't. And she asked if Tommy had read some book she'd written. She seemed a bit up-tight because he'd said something at lunch that sounded as if he had, but I didn't see how he could have done if it wasn't even published yet."

"He could have read the typescript," Lambert suggested.

"If he did, he didn't mention it to me," Carole said. "I think he was pretending he'd read it because the others were talking about it and he didn't like being left out. He hated being left out of anything."

It was curious how the book kept cropping up, Lambert thought. Because of it Alethea had been invited here for the weekend to meet Gillian Lane; Boston had implied he had read it when almost certainly he hadn't; and after lunch the Lanes had had a fairly heated discussion about it in the garden. A discussion which had ended with Lane stumping off to the Wheatsheaf alone.

Surely it couldn't have anything to do with the murder. Alethea Wightman and Chester had both read it, and neither of them had suggested it contained anything which might provide a link. It seemed unlikely they and the author would all keep quiet if there were anything. And why, if there were a connection, should Boston be the one to be killed? Lambert suspected the book was a red herring.

"How long did you stay out there talking?" he enquired.

Carole thought for a moment. "I don't know. About twenty minutes, I suppose."

That tallied with what Chester had said. "And then?"

"I wondered what Tommy was doing. He couldn't still be on the phone, it was three quarters of an hour." For the first time the girl's voice faltered. "I came in to see where he was."

Gently Lambert asked, "Was the study the first place you looked for him, Mrs. Boston?"

"Yes."

"Why there?"

"I don't know. It just seemed the obvious place. He'd been on the phone in there, and it was downstairs. If he hadn't been in the study, I expect I'd have looked up in our bedroom." Carole spoke quietly, her voice under control again.

"And you found the door was locked?"

"Yes."

"You tried it?"

"Yes."

"Did you call out?"

"I—I think so. Yes. Yes, I know I did."

Carole said she knew of nobody who might

have wanted her husband dead. "A lot of people didn't like him. I know that. But . . ." Her voice nearly broke again, but after a second or two she continued, "He didn't see what he was doing when he talked like he did. He caused trouble sometimes. But killing him . . . ! I think sometimes he was afraid. Afraid he was slipping, that he wouldn't get another series. And that he was getting old. He'd *seemed* older lately. And he'd changed. Before we were married he was kind and thoughtful. He used to give me presents suddenly, for no reason except that he enjoyed doing it. Not expensive things, I don't mean. He hadn't done that for a long while." Carole stopped.

Lambert waited a little while, then he took her through some of the points in her story again.

"I'm afraid we may have to see you again later," he told her, "but that's all for the present."

It was hard to say if she was distressed by her husband's death, he thought when she had gone. If not, that didn't mean she had murdered him. Nor that she knew who had.

Susan was worried. Mainly what troubled her

was the question Lambert had asked: if Boston was so disliked by everybody, why had Logan invited him for the weekend? But there were other things, things she was reluctant to admit, even to herself. One was the suspicion that Logan had really been asking Carole, and Boston had been invited only because he had to be.

All right, Susan told herself, what if Logan had wanted Carole? It was his affair and nothing to do with her. Why should she concern herself?

He was all the things she had always disliked in a man, vain, egotistical, pushing. And he thrived on making mischief. Not real trouble between people, but stirring up things to see what would happen. So why did she try to pretend he wasn't really like that?

It was true she knew him better than most people did. She knew he could be kind and generous, and his string of conquests was largely a myth. He was like a small boy cocking a snook at the world. Or a perpetual student who refused to accept that he and that world had changed since he was twenty-one. No wonder his wife had divorced him years ago.

None of which helped Susan's dilemma at all.

You silly little fool, she told herself. You love him.

She was angry, with herself and with Fate. After her experience with Jeremy she had vowed she wouldn't allow herself to become emotionally involved with any man for a long, long time. That was one reason why she had left a perfectly good job she enjoyed, but which meant her seeing Jeremy at least twice a day, to be Logan's secretary; she had seen him on television and disliked him. Working for him, she had told herself, she could remain cool and efficient, her emotions intact. Also there had been the appeal of a job on the fringes of a new, fascinating world, and being close enough to help Frank and Nina with Simon at weekends.

Now, she told herself, you're hoist with your own petard, and serve you right. She wasn't quite sure what a petard was. Some sort of explosive, she believed. Which didn't seem very suitable for being hoisted on. More like blown up by. But perhaps she had got it wrong.

She was perfectly well aware that Chester regarded her merely as a capable and reliable secretary. A sort of word processor with a brain. He might have found working with her less pleasant if she had been fat, dowdy and fifty, but basically it wouldn't have made any difference. To him she was a piece of office equipment.

Susan didn't know which would be worse, for him to know how she felt or for him never to know and go on treating her as if she were part of the furniture.

She wondered sometimes what he got up to when he was at the university. He had had a group of his students to stay during the Easter vacation and it was obvious the girls doted on him. They were like moon-struck calves, the little fools. But was she any better? And she was twenty-eight, old enough to be sensible.

Heaven help me, she thought. And Logan, too, now. That superintendent looked intelligent, he must be wondering about the reason for this weekend's party. As guests Alethea and the Lanes called for no explanation. Nor did Peter Hastings, he was a writer and knew Logan fairly well. But the Bostons . . . Susan couldn't rid herself of a nagging fear that Logan had had some compelling reason for inviting them.

I shouldn't feel like this, she told herself. If I love him, I should have faith in him. How can I even think of him killing anybody? But love wasn't blind. Not hers, at any rate; she could see his faults and love him despite them.

The thought persisted that if he had planned a crime this was how he would have done it, with all the seeming impossibilities and confusions. He would have revelled in them.

"What are you thinking about?"

She hadn't heard him come up behind her and she started. "Oh, lots of things," she answered lightly.

"Alethea's going. Lambert says he doesn't need her any more now, and she can't get away fast enough. I wondered if you'd be a darling and run her to the station. She's just got time to catch the seven forty-three if you go now."

"Yes, of course I will," Susan agreed. "What's happening about Carole?"

"I don't know. I don't think she fancies going home, and I can't very well suggest she stays here, can I?"

Poor Logan, Susan thought. It was typical of him to worry about a thing like that; he could be surprisingly conventional at times. But he was right, of course. Apart from the gossip there was bound to be in the village, if the papers got to know . . .

The papers. She hadn't thought of them

before. The reporters would be here soon, descending like a pack of wolves on Frewley Green, prying into all their private lives, scavenging for any scraps of dirt they could find.

"Who's to know?" she asked lightly, banishing thoughts of the Press until they appeared.

"You can't be serious." Chester sounded so shocked she wanted to laugh. It's nerves, she told herself.

"All right, whose business is it of anybody but you and Carole? I doubt if the old dears in the village would suspect you of forcing your evil intentions on her tonight."

Susan saw the expression that appeared fleetingly in his eyes before he smiled and knew she shouldn't have said that. It was rude and in bad taste. And it wasn't the sort of thing she said. Logan had looked startled and—yes, disappointed. Oh Lord! she thought miserably.

"I'm sorry," she apologized. "You know what I mean."

Suddenly Chester grinned. "She might not want to stay. There's always the Lamb at Breckley—or somewhere in Wittenham, if she'd rather."

Susan wondered if he was waiting for her to

suggest the girl stay with her. Well, she wasn't going to. It might not be very Christian, but she couldn't.

"What about her family?" she asked. "Hasn't she got anybody she can go to, or who can come here?"

"I don't know," Chester admitted. "You take Alethea to the station and I'll see what's to be done."

Susan thought she could picture him playing the sympathetic older friend, helpful and understanding. The trouble was, he wouldn't be acting.

Lambert, Roger Beeley and Flick were in Lambert's room at Divisional HQ, a modern red brick and glass building on the outskirts of Wittenham. There might be interview rooms and cells inside; externally it looked like just another office block, and while it hadn't done much for the crime figures, it was a lot more pleasant to work in than the Victorian building in the High Street it had replaced.

"From what we know so far," Lambert said, "it seems Boston was killed by a single thrust from behind with an ordinary kitchen knife some time between two thirty-two, when

Chester saw the study door open and no one there, and three oh three, when Chester and Lane looked through the window and saw him lying by the desk. It's on the cards Chester's lying, but what he says ties in with Dr. Felstead's idea of when Boston died. There's no way he can have killed himself, we can rule out accident, and there were no prints on the knife. So it must have been murder."

The others nodded assent.

"Only he can't have been murdered, because the room was as good as sealed on the inside, and the murderer couldn't have got out."

"It can't have been sealed," Beeley objected.

"Exactly." Lambert's tone was heavy with irony; Beeley had a gift for stating the obvious. "Whoever killed him must have got out before the door was locked."

"Why should anybody else lock it?" Flick wanted to know. "And how did they get out?"

Beeley gave her a sour look. The super encouraged kids who didn't know a palm-print from a fortune-teller to come out with their half-baked ideas. Women had a role in the force, but in Beeley's opinion it should be limited to dealing with delinquent girls and minor traffic offences. CID was men's work.

"It's like a bloody detective story," he grumbled.

Logan had been thinking much the same, and he had taken the notion a step further. Logan Chester was not only an authority on detective stories, he was an enthusiast; his book and the collection in his study were evidence of that. Moreover it seemed certain the murder had been planned in advance, and everything pointed to the murderer having that sort of interest. Chester was probably enough of an egotist to believe he could get away with it. He would have enjoyed pitting his wits against those of the police, and who else would have come up with that hoary old chestnut of crime fiction, the locked room?

But was he enough of a gambler? And was he capable of cold-blooded murder? Come to that, had he either motive or opportunity? There was a lot more digging to be done before they knew who had and who hadn't possessed a motive; opportunity was something else.

"This looks like being one of those cases where the most important factor is time," Lambert said. "We've got to account for every minute. So look at the timetable according to their accounts of what they were doing." He sifted one sheet from his sheaf of papers and passed it across his desk.

Heads close together, Beeley and Flick read:

2:10	Lunch finished. Elsie Hemmings starts clearing table. Boston says he must make phone call.
2:14	Lanes go out to garden.
2:15	Boston goes to study. Susan Wareham says she is going to post office and Miss Rider's. Followed out by Mrs. Boston, who goes to study door, then up to their room.
2:17	Elsie Hemmings comes to dining-room to say she is going home. Miss Wightman goes up to her room.
2:18	Hastings goes to pub to fetch his pipe. Chester goes out to garden but doesn't talk to Lanes.
2:25 approx.	Hastings leaves pub and walks round to lawn. Doesn't go through the house. Lane leaves his wife and goes to pub via drawing-room.
2:27 approx.	Hastings joins Mrs. Lane on lawn. Lane arrives at pub.

2:32	Chester goes to kitchen and sees study door open. No one in study.
2:34 approx.	Mrs. Boston comes out of house and joins Mrs. Lane and Hastings.
2:40	Miss Wareham returns. Finds side door stuck and goes round to kitchen door. Helps Chester with drinks.
2:45 approx.	They take drinks out to others on lawn.
3:00	Mrs. Boston goes to find her husband.
3:02	Returns to say study door locked and no answer.
3:03	Chester meets Lane coming out by French windows. They try study door, then go round to
3:04	look in at study window. Hastings joins them from lawn.
3:05	Hastings goes to call doctor. Chester climbs in. Lane watches him, then goes to tell those on lawn what has happened.

"Those times may not be exact, but they're

as near as we're likely to get," Lambert told them when they had had time to study the sheet.

"If they're telling the truth, it must have been Lane, the Wightman woman or Chester," Beeley said. "The others were together on the lawn."

"What about Mrs. Boston?" Flick suggested. "She could have done it before she joined them. And, after all, she probably stood to gain more than anybody."

"You think she could have killed him, fixed the locked door and windows and gone outside as if nothing had happened in two minutes flat?" Beeley's tone was scathing. "And with Chester just across the hall in the kitchen?"

"I was only thinking aloud, Sarge," Flick told him, not one whit abashed. "I admit it doesn't seem very likely."

"Too right it doesn't."

"Nor does the case against Chester, on the face of it," Lambert commented. "For much the same reasons. There was eight minutes when he was alone in the kitchen before Miss Wareham came back. That would have been ample time for him to stab Boston and set up the rest of it if he'd got it all worked out beforehand. But would he have risked it, knowing she was likely to come in at any minute? As it was, she was gone longer than she expected." Lambert paused. "Still, maybe it wasn't such a risk. He knew the woman at the post office and the old lady, Miss Rider, he could be pretty sure they'd both keep Miss Wareham talking for several minutes. With most of the others settled on the lawn, and Miss Wightman at work upstairs, he would be less likely to be seen slipping in and out of the study than you might think."

"He can't have planned it in advance," Beeley objected. "He wouldn't know Boston would be in the study just then."

"That doesn't mean the murderer didn't have it all worked out. He must have thought of a way of persuading Boston to go there—and that points to Chester, it was his house and his party. When Boston went of his own free will, it made the job easier."

"And Chester told him to use that phone," Flick pointed out.

"Yes."

"It's funny so many of them are writers," Beeley remarked. "Boston claimed he was,

Chester is, and so are Hastings and Mrs. Lane. And Miss Wightman's a publisher."

"Which is nearly as bad," Lambert agreed solemnly. "What about it?"

"Well, whoever killed Boston didn't just stick a knife in him and scarper like an ordinary person would, they had to fix up the locked room. It's the sort of thing murderers do in books, just to make it all more complicated. Most people wouldn't think like that. If only one of them was a writer, it would point to him, but when so many of them are . . ." Beeley looked disgusted.

"Authors are ordinary people," Lambert protested, grinning. "And don't forget, millions of people read mystery stories. They can get ideas." Beeley might have a point, he thought, but he wasn't wholly convinced, even though he had been thinking on similar lines himself.

"I don't see it's funny they're all writers," Flick said. "I mean, they're the sort of people Logan Chester would know. I bet most of your friends are in the force, Sarge."

Lambert smiled. "*Touché*, Roger." There were times when Beeley was a little too pleased with himself, and he didn't mind Flick deflating him, as long as she didn't go too far.

147

The sergeant didn't look pleased. "It still doesn't make things any easier," he said. "There's no proof Miss Wightman was up in her room all the time, and it doesn't seem very likely she'd stay there the whole afternoon on a day like this."

"I'm not so sure," Lambert told him. "She's not the outdoor type, and if she wanted to get on with her work without being disturbed or having to talk to people, her room would be the best place. There's another thing: after what happened this morning she probably wanted to keep out of Boston's way."

"Do you really think he tried to kiss her, sir?" Flick asked, smiling broadly. "That doesn't seem very likely either."

"That's because you're young. Why should she lie about it? A kiss in the bushes from Boston's hardly the sort of thing Alethea Wightman would boast about, she's too fond of her dignity. And two or three other people saw him clutching the side of his head. Mrs. Boston says he came into the house muttering about 'That bloody bitch,' and there was no other woman around. It's only a guess, but I'd say he did it on the spur of the moment, knowing she'd be furious. He seems to have had that sort of sense of humour."

"Urghh!" Flick grimaced.

"If it wasn't her, it must have been either Lane or Chester," Beeley said. He didn't like digressions, they confused the issues, and what happened between Alethea Wightman and the dead man in the garden hours before in his opinion almost certainly had nothing to do with the murder. A woman didn't kill a man merely because he'd kissed her. Not even such an odd one as the publisher.

"It may have been her," Lambert told him. "All I said was, it's not as unlikely as you may think, her preferring to spend the afternoon in her room. She could still have slipped down and killed Boston. But for some other reason, not because of what happened in the garden."

"Lane went into the house," Beeley remarked. "He could have done it before he went across to the pub."

"Not unless Chester is lying about the study door being open when he went to get the drinks; Lane had gone by then. And if he didn't stab Boston, why should he lie? I'm more interested in what Lane did later. What did the landlord have to say?"

Beeley took out his notebook and flipped through the pages. "Hastings got there just before closing time," he reported. "Jarman, the landlord, couldn't say exactly when, but he reckons it must have been two twenty-five. He asked if anybody had found his pipe. Jarman told him they hadn't, and he looked round. It was on a window sill by where they'd all been sitting before lunch."

"Did anybody else see it there?" Lambert enquired.

"It was one of the other customers spotted it," Beeley replied. "Hastings was only there a minute or two."

"And Lane?"

"He came in just after Hastings had gone. According to Mrs. Jarman, he was in an ugly mood, ready to start a row with anybody. He had a double scotch, and by the time he'd drunk it it was past closing-time. He left with the last of the stragglers."

"What time was that?"

"A quarter to three."

Lambert looked thoughtful. "So what was Lane doing between two forty-five and three?" he asked.

9

THE other two stared at him.

"I want you to dig up everything you can about all of them except Alethea Wightman, Roger," he said. "Leave her to me. Tomlin can give you a hand, he's finished that credit-card enquiry at Dancombe. You know the drill."

"Right, sir," Beeley said.

"I'll ask Inspector Fletcher to put somebody onto tracing the call Boston made, but it's one in a million he'll turn up anything."

Flick was studying the timetable again. "Miss Wareham could have got back earlier than she says," she observed.

"She could," Lambert agreed. "I don't suppose we'll be able to tie the people at the post office or Miss Rider down to any exact times, but, according to her, the side door was sticking and she had to go round to the back and in by the kitchen door. She can't have gone that way before because Chester would have seen her. And the same objection applies to her as to Mrs. Boston: would she have risked killing Boston in the study, and arranging the locked door and windows with him in the kitchen? But we'll have to check that door and see if it really does stick."

Beeley's thoughts were following different lines. "Boston must have been pretty well off," he remarked. "Does his wife get everything?"

"I don't know," Lambert replied. "I haven't been able to get hold of his solicitor yet. People shouldn't commit murders at weekends."

"I wouldn't put it past her to stick a knife in him."

"She can't have done," Flick objected. "You said yourself, she only had two minutes."

Beeley gave her a look calculated to kill on the spot any ambition she might harbour of being the brains of the CID. "Rule her out and you're back to the Wightman woman, Lane and Chester," he said.

"It looks like it," Lambert agreed. He had a feeling they wouldn't get much farther until they knew how the murderer had escaped from a room where the door was locked on the inside and both windows securely fastened. He had even considered the possibility that he—or she—might have waited, concealed somewhere in the study, until Chester climbed in. But Lane and Chester were both adamant there had been no one there, and, anyway, where could the murderer have hidden? There were no cupboards in the study, only the bookshelves, the desk, a filing cabinet and three chairs. No trapdoors in the floor or hiding places concealed behind the shelves. Even Alethea Wightman, thin as she was, couldn't have hidden herself there. No, somehow the murderer, having killed Boston, had escaped from the room, leaving it effectively sealed.

Lambert told himself it was too reminiscent of the Yellow Room and John Dickson Carr. Which brought him back to Chester, the authority on detective stories.

Only he, Miss Wightman or Lane, it seemed, could be guilty. True, Susan Wareham and the dead man's widow had both been alone briefly at different times during the crucial half-hour, but Lambert couldn't see either of them as the killer. Not only for the reasons he had explained to Beeley and Flick, but because no one planning a crime so carefully would have relied as much on chance as they would have had to do.

None of the three had an obvious motive, but it might be merely a case of digging and one would be found. In the meantime, tomorrow he should know the results of the post mortem. Although what more they would tell him he had no idea.

For the dozenth time Gillian told herself she had to know. This evening Trevor had accused her of believing he had killed Tommy Boston and she had denied it. But the uncertainty and fear remained, making a barrier between them, and although putting the question into words might endanger all she was trying to salvage, she had to risk that. Suspicion would be even more harmful.

Outside it was dark, and no glimmer of light showed between the curtains. Beside her Trevor was asleep. She turned over, slid her legs out from under the duvet and padded silently across to the window. At first she could see nothing. Then, as her eyes grew accustomed to the near-darkness, she could make out the silhouettes of the trees at the bottom of the garden.

It was so peaceful, she thought, the air so mild, without a breath of wind to stir the leaves. So normal it was hard to remember that only a few hours ago a man she knew had been stabbed to death within a few yards of where she was sitting, killed by somebody else she knew.

While that might be hard to accept, the consequences were real enough and they looked like destroying her security. Gillian craved reassurance and she felt dreadfully alone.

Trevor's way of life, which at first she had shared enthusiastically because it was different from anything she had known before, had come to seem second-rate and his friends philistine and common. He had gone along with her love of riding and bought horses for them both. He even seemed to enjoy it himself, although he was a poor horseman. But he cared nothing for things which were important to her like books and the theatre, while the only music he would admit to enjoying was the pop rubbish of ten and twenty years ago.

To be fair, he had never tried to stop her enjoying the things she liked, and there were still things they did share. Their love of this house for one. Perhaps I'm just restless, Gillian thought. We've been married eight years, the first phase is over and I've got to adjust to the next. We both have.

And now, out of the blue, this had come to threaten everything.

Just along the landing Carole was in one of the spare bedrooms. She had dreaded the prospect of going back alone to her home on the other side of Breckley, and as it was too late for her parents to come from Kent, Gillian had suggested she spend tonight here. Was she asleep? she wondered. Or tossing and turning, haunted by what had happened? She couldn't have loved Boston, did she care very much that he was dead?

"What are you doing?" Trevor demanded sleepily from the bed.

Gillian started; she hadn't known he was awake. "Just looking out," she answered.

"You can't see anything, it's too dark."

"I can a little. It's a lovely night."

"Come back to bed."

Gillian let the curtain fall back into place, but she didn't move. It called for a good deal of will-power to ask, "Trevor, where were you this afternoon when you said you were at the pub?"

"I told you, that's where I was." He was wide awake now.

"You can't have been there all the time, it was past three when you came back." Trevor said nothing and Gillian went on, "You knew Tommy Boston before yesterday, didn't you?"

There was a noticeable pause before Trevor asked, "How did you know?"

That repulsive little man! Alethea told herself. She cringed mentally when she thought about his behaviour yesterday and her humiliation when she knew Logan Chester had seen her in his arms. Decent people shouldn't be expected to tolerate such creatures; she was glad he was dead.

She felt no anxiety for herself. That superintendent—Latchford was his name? No, Lambert—hadn't struck her as very impressive. But what could one ask of a provincial policeman? It would be unreasonable to expect him to understand writers and people like her and Logan Chester. Not that she minded that. On the contrary, it suited her very well.

Alethea told herself bitterly she owed it all to Logan. He had invited her for this appalling weekend. What on earth had led her to accept?

She regretted she had had no opportunity for a longer talk to Gillian Lane. She had been filled with admiration for the way Gillian had dealt with Boston's uncouth behaviour at lunch, but after that the younger woman had slightly disappointed her. She was obviously well bred, as well as perceptive and able to write well—how rarely the first went with the third and fourth, Alethea reflected—but she appeared to be wrapped up in that boorish husband of hers. Her novel was clearly autobiographical—which probably meant she had put all she had in her into it and she would never write anything else nearly as good again. Nevertheless it was definitely worth publishing.

Alethea laid down the book about Japan she had been reading. She approved of the Japanese, they had a practical approach to life. To death, too.

I can't feel sorry he's dead, Carole told herself. I know it's wrong, but I can't help it. And I don't feel guilty.

He cheated me. I thought it would be lovely being married to him, and I did love him in a sort of way, whatever they think, but it was awful, knowing people hated him and being afraid all the time what he'd say next. He wasn't really afraid he was slipping, he was too conceited for that. So why did I make excuses for him?

I'm glad I didn't tell anybody he said he was going to make a new will. He can't have known about Peter and me, can he? I wonder how much I'll get.

Peter Hastings lay awake a long time, unable to sleep. He couldn't believe what had happened.

Logan Chester, as usual, slept soundly.

The morning was much cooler than the previous day. Clouds which had blown up during the night had brought a light rain with them and when Susan looked out of her bedroom window just after seven-thirty the asphalt surface of the street outside was gleaming wet and raindrops were falling into the puddles. Telling herself the farmers and the gardens needed rain, she went along the hall to her bathroom.

Her flat occupied the upper floor of a two-storey detached house. The largest of the four bedrooms was now her living-room and the smallest her kitchen. Since the departure of her flat-mate the third bedroom was used only for occasional visitors and a wall with a front door in it had been erected across the old landing. It provided her with a tiny hall and the privacy she valued.

Today was Sunday, she thought. She had offered to go over to Forge Cottage if Logan wanted her to, and half hoped he would. It would show he wanted her there and, more prosaically, it would help keep her mind off what had happened yesterday to be working. But he hadn't, and uncharacteristically she felt restless, not knowing what to do with herself until this afternoon, when she would go as usual to look after Simon while Nina and Frank went out. It was the only chance they had to go out together during the week. Looking after a nine-year-old boy who could do nothing for himself and not even speak intelligibly was a terrible strain for the most loving parents.

Thinking about her nephew brought Susan's thoughts back to Tommy Boston. She felt no sorrow, she told herself defiantly. He had got what he deserved and she was glad he was dead. At least now he couldn't wreck other people's lives.

Susan knew her restlessness was caused less by her having nothing in particular to do— there were several letters she should write and half a dozen jobs to be done round the flat— than by the uncertainty. She supposed it would always be like this until the police arrested somebody.

Even then that wouldn't be the end of it. There would follow with grim inevitability the magistrates' hearing, the trial and, not the end but only the end of the beginning, the only possible sentence.

She thrust the thought aside.

The police couldn't suspect Logan, could they? She had told the superintendent she returned to the house at twenty to three, but that wasn't true. She believed it at the time, it was only after she got home and switched on the television news she found her watch was five minutes slow. It meant she hadn't got back from the post office and seeing Miss Rider until two forty-five, and Logan had been alone in the kitchen five minutes longer than she had led the police to believe. Nearly a quarter of an hour.

He couldn't have been getting the fruit cup all that time, could he? When she came in he hadn't done much at all. But if not, what was he doing? For at least the tenth time in the last few hours Susan told herself it was unthinkable he could have had anything to do with Tommy Boston's murder. She wouldn't even consider the possibility, it was too horrible.

But unthinkable or not, her anxiety persisted.

And like the anxiety, something else, something half remembered, nagged at her brain. She thought that if she didn't try to remember, sometime when she was thinking about something else it would come back to her.

Buttoning up her shirt, she pulled on a pair of trousers, tidied her hair and went across the hall to her kitchen. Would the superintendent want to see her again? If he did, she would have to tell him about her mistake over the time. She should tell him anyway, shouldn't she? Not wait until he asked her more questions. If he had to drag it out of her then, it would assume an importance it didn't merit. He was bound to ask himself why she hadn't told him as soon as she remembered and think the worst. The police always did, didn't they?

It's too early to ring him yet, she told herself. I'll leave it until later.

Almost without thinking what she was doing, she took a packet of cereal from a cupboard, shook some of its contents into a bowl and poured on the top off a pint of milk. Then, picking up the bowl and a spoon, she carried them into her living-room.

As she pulled out a chair to sit at the table

she suddenly remembered what it was that had been niggling in her brain. It was something Logan had said after they joined the others on the lawn with the drinks. He had asked where everybody was and when they told him he commented, "So that's everyone accounted for then." At the time it had struck her as a strange thing to say, now it seemed to acquire a dreadful significance. It suggested he had been checking up on where the members of the party were at that precise moment—and he would only have done that if he knew something had happened. Something like Tommy Boston's being murdered.

If anyone had asked Susan twenty-four hours ago how well she knew Logan Chester she would have answered "Very well." Now she was no longer sure. He hid so successfully behind his public image that sometimes she wondered if anyone really understood him— including Logan. Now she forced herself to consider the possibility that he had stabbed Boston—her mind baulked at "murdered"— and knew the answer was "I don't know." Perhaps Boston's death had been an accident, they had struggled and the comedian had fallen on the knife. Wasn't that what people always claimed when they were accused of a stabbing? Perhaps it really did happen. But she knew she was deceiving herself, his death had been no accident. The murderer's taking the knife into the study and the locked door proved that.

What reason could Logan have had for wanting Boston dead? The answer, Susan told herself miserably, was only too clear. It was a matter of history that the comedian had nearly wrecked one of Logan's television programmes, departing from the outline they had agreed and doing everything he could to score off him and make him look ridiculous. Not only had Boston's fans enjoyed seeing Logan Chester cut down to size, there had been some nasty comments in one or two of the papers, and the producer had been furious until he saw that the incident was the best advertisement the programme could have had. It actually climbed into the ratings for the next two weeks.

Surprisingly, Logan had seemed to take it all in good part. In truth he had had no grounds for complaining, what had been done to him wasn't very different from what he had planned to do to Boston, only the comedian had got in first. He was an old hand, perhaps he had seen Logan's intentions and forestalled him. Anyhow, that had seemed to be the end of it, they went for a drink together after recording the programme and, at least on the surface, there was no ill feeling. But Susan knew Logan had more than his share of vanity; he must have furiously resented what Boston had done to him.

She was astonished when he told her he had invited him and his wife to Forge Cottage for the weekend. She had had her own reasons for being appalled, but Logan's motives still concerned her. Usually he was far more fastidious in his choice of guests.

Again she wondered if it had been Carole he really wanted to come. And now something new occurred to her: was it possible Logan had planned to revenge himself on Boston through his wife? Oh no! she thought. He wouldn't. It showed how mixed up and afraid she was that she should even imagine such a thing.

Who could have stabbed Boston? If what they said was true, and none of them had gone indoors, it couldn't have been any of the party on the lawn. Trevor Lane hadn't been with them, he had gone off by himself earlier and not returned until Boston was dead. Could he . . . ? Susan could imagine him losing his temper and lashing out.

She finished her cereal, took the bowl out to the kitchen and made herself some coffee. Should she phone the police now? No, she decided, leave it a little longer.

Taking her coffee back to the living-room, she considered what she should do when she had drunk it. Before all this happened she had planned to give this room a good going over today, but now the prospect was very unappealing.

At the same moment Susan was thinking about turning out her living-room, Logan Chester woke and reached out for the clock on his bedside table. It said nineteen minutes past eight.

He picked up the book he had been reading last night, read for a quarter of an hour, then got up. On the whole, he thought as he shaved, things hadn't gone too badly. The danger was by no means over—indeed, he suspected the worst was still to come—but so far so reasonably good.

The superintendent, Lambert, hadn't seemed a fool, but policemen suffered from a fundamental handicap, they lacked imagination. And it would take a good deal of imagination to solve this case.

Chester wondered why Lambert's name should bother him. It wasn't so very uncommon, of course, but it seemed to him he had heard it quite recently in some other connection. He tried to remember, but whatever it was eluded him, and in the end he gave up and went downstairs.

It was his custom on Sunday mornings to walk across the green before breakfast to fetch his papers from the post office, and he saw no reason to break with it today. There were three men in the shop talking to Alec Rayment when he walked in. The conversation stopped when they saw him and he knew they were wary, uncertain whether to regard him as a victim of circumstance or as a possible murderer. Either way he was an object of curiosity.

For the first time he noticed a small display of hardware just inside the door with, at its centre, a board on which was mounted a range of kitchen knives. There were four of them in order of size below the manufacturer's name. Two, the second and third largest, were missing. He hesitated momentarily, but even

Chester hadn't the courage or effrontery to stop to examine them more closely.

He took his papers and carried them back to his house, conscious of four pairs of eyes watching him. Letting himself in by the side door, he entered the study, experiencing a second's revulsion as he did so. And though it passed immediately, nevertheless he avoided looking at the floor by his desk as he crossed to one of the bookshelves on the wall opposite the door. A cool breeze was blowing in through the damaged window and he told himself he must nail some hardboard over it after breakfast. There was no hope of getting a man to fix a new pane until tomorrow at the earliest.

When he had found the book he wanted he carried it into the kitchen. He had eaten practically nothing since lunch yesterday and he suddenly realized he was hungry.

When he had cooked himself breakfast and eaten it he found in a drawer in the study a packet of tie on luggage labels. Armed with them and a ball-point pen, he went round the house, removing the keys from every door and labelling them. Only one was missing, that to the smallest bedroom which he used as a store-room. As far as he could remember, there had been no key to that door for as long as he had owned the house. When he had collected all the others he tried them, one after the other, in the lock of the study door.

There were only two still left when he found one which not only fitted the lock but turned it. It was the key to the bedroom Alethea Wightman had occupied on Friday night.

He tried the last one, but it wouldn't go into the keyhole, let alone operate the lock. With a rather grim smile of satisfaction, Chester returned the keys to the doors from which he had taken them, removed the labels and went back to the drawing-room. There he sat down in his favourite easy chair and thought.

10

SUSAN was right in thinking Lambert wouldn't be at his office early. The previous evening he had telephoned from Forge Cottage giving instructions for a man to be sent round to the public library to borrow a copy of Boston's autobiography, and last night in bed he had started reading it. This morning he had woken soon after six and carried on.

As he had expected, there was nothing overt to show that anybody else had collaborated in writing the book, which was profusely illustrated with photographs of Boston on stage, accompanied by other celebrities, or with one or other of his four wives. The first was a girl he had known only a month before they married. He was then twenty-two. That marriage had lasted thirteen years, and perhaps it was coincidence that Boston had just begun to be successful when he divorced her. Neither his second nor his third marriage had lasted nearly as long.

Lambert found the book mildly unpleasant.

Boston's self-satisfaction ran right through it; there were no stories against him, always he was the "good guy" or the one who succeeded where others failed. Lambert wondered if that was Hastings' doing and, if so, whether it was deliberate. Most people reading the book would finish it with a pretty poor opinion of Boston; was that his revenge on a man he clearly detested? On the other hand, it could have been inevitable, given the material the comedian had provided him with. After all, Boston must have read the typescript and approved it before it went to the publishers, so presumably it was what he wanted.

Lambert put the book down, got out of bed and dressed. It contained no clue to what Boston thought or felt, nor what was behind his public face. If anything was. It was the usual cliché-ridden biography of a show-business star, all surface and no depth. Apart from his overweening egotism the man remained a shadow. There wasn't even much showbiz glitter; the writing was competent but dull. Lambert was surprised that a firm with the standing of Alethea Wightman's should have published it.

After a hurried breakfast of toast and coffee

he got out his car and drove to his office. Beeley and Flick were already there.

"I've been reading Boston's book," he explained. "As far as I can see, there's nothing in it to help us."

"Inspector Fletcher's had no luck yet tracing his call," Beeley told him.

Lambert grunted. It was only what he had expected. How easy it must have been, he thought, when every village had its manual telephone exchange and, as operator, an old tabby with nothing to do but listen in to people's calls. But perhaps it had never really been like that. Now, if life became much more automated, they would be able to leave solving crimes entirely to computers. Feed in the facts and out would come the solution. Instant, infallible detection. When that happened, people like Beeley and him would be redundant.

"Have either of you any ideas about the locked room?" he asked.

"How do you mean, sir?" Beeley wanted to know.

"Anything at all. I have a feeling why it was done is as important as how."

"But we know that, don't we?" Flick looked puzzled. "I mean, it was to make us think whoever killed Boston couldn't have done it. That nobody could. I know that sounds muddled—"

"It does," Beeley agreed brutally.

Flick managed a rueful grin and Lambert laughed.

"Perhaps," he agreed. "Or it may have been done simply to complicate things. It must have taken at least two or three minutes to set it up, even with everything worked out in advance, and every second entailed additional risk for the murderer. So he must have had a pretty compelling reason for going to all that trouble. If we knew what that reason was, we would be a long way forward." Lambert paused. "I'm going to see the daily woman, Elsie Hemmings, and Chester again. You'd better come with me, Miss Graham."

Beeley studiously avoided looking at either of them. Miss Graham! he thought disgustedly. She was a constable, not the chief constable's daughter. But if the boss wanted to take her along for the sake of her company, it was no business of his.

"I'll get on with that checking on the guests," he said, standing up.

Lambert nodded. "Boston's solicitor may

come up with something that gives one of them a motive; so far there doesn't seem a convincing reason for any of them to kill him. Except his widow."

It took Lambert and Flick half an hour to cover the few miles to Frewley Green. Whatever Beeley imagined, for most of the time Lambert drove in silence and Flick occupied herself with her own thoughts. They had nothing to do with the case, being mainly concerned with her boyfriend and whether she would finish in time to meet him that evening.

It was still too early for people to be going to church, and the village seemed almost deserted as they drove along the street.

"Do you know the number?" Lambert asked.

"Twenty-two, sir," Flick replied. She had looked it up in case he should ask as soon as they got into the car.

Number 22 was one of a row of adjoining colour-washed cottages with lowering thatch roofs and ancient square casement windows. At some of them the upper storeys overhung the narrow pavement.

"Picturesque," Lambert commented, stopping the car.

"Probably inconvenient, too," Flick added.

"The trouble with women," Lambert told her, "is that they have no aesthetic sense. They reduce everything to a matter of housekeeping."

"That's because they have to do the housework, sir."

Lambert laughed. "Come on."

There was no bell, and Elsie answered his knock almost at once. She stood in the doorway regarding them with obvious suspicion.

"Miss Hemmings?" Lambert said.

"Yes?" It was as much a challenge as a reply, and in any case hardly forthcoming.

"We're police, Miss Hemmings. I'm Detective Superintendent Lambert and this is WPC Graham."

"I suppose it's to do with what 'appened at Mr. Chester's yesterday afternoon," Elsie said.

"That's right. We'd like to ask you a few questions. May we come in?"

Nasty things happened these days, people worming their way into your house, Elsie thought. She'd always said she'd be very careful before she left anybody into hers, whoever they said they were.

"'Ave you got a card or something that says you're 'oo you say you are?" she demanded.

"You're quite right," Lambert said, producing proof of his identity and trying not to let his amusement show.

Apparently satisfied, Elsie opened the door wide enough for him and Flick to step into a small, meticulously clean room rather crowded with old, shabby and no doubt treasured pieces of furniture.

"You'd best sit down," she said grudgingly, herself sitting on an upright chair and turning it to face them. "What do you want to ask me then?"

Lambert, feeling rather like a small boy confronted by a formidable and disapproving headmistress, took her through what she knew of the events of the previous day from her arrival at Forge Cottage just after eleven o'clock until she left.

"What time was that?" he asked.

"Seventeen minutes past two."

"You're sure?"

"Of course I'm sure. I looked. Mr. Chester pays me by the hour, and I always make a note of when I get there and when I leave. I like to keep things straight. Mind you, mostly it's the same times, but special days like yesterday, then I write it down."

"And you went into the dining-room to tell him you were going?" Lambert said. Elsie nodded. "Did you see anybody in the hall?"

"Only that Mrs. Boston coming away from the study and going towards the stairs. Miss Wareham 'ad gone out. Oh, and I met Miss Wightman or whatever 'er name is in the doorway. She nearly knocked me over, but she didn't say a word of sorry."

Elsie looked more disapproving than aggrieved, Lambert thought. "Who was in the dining-room then?" he asked.

"Mr. Chester an' that Mr. 'Astings as lives just up the road." Elsie almost sniffed.

"You don't like Mr. Hastings?" Lambert ventured.

"I don't know 'im." Elsie paused, then added mysteriously, "Our ways aren't all the same, I've learnt that."

"So you don't approve of him?"

"It's not for me to approve or disapprove," Elsie retorted. "I just don't think it's right for a single man to 'ave married women in 'is 'ouse like that."

"Mr. Hastings does?" Lambert asked. "Married women from the village?"

"No, that Mrs. Boston. 'Er with all 'er dyed

'air an' paint. I saw 'er coming out of 'is 'ouse th' other afternoon. Looking very pleased with 'erself, she was. It didn't take much to know what—" Elsie stopped abruptly.

Behind Lambert Flick blew her nose noisily. He took out a large photograph of the knife which had killed Boston and showed it to Elsie.

"Do you recognize that knife?" he asked her.

"I s'pose it's the one what was used to kill 'im." She studied the picture without showing any signs of horror. "It looks like an ordin'ry kitchen knife to me."

"It is," Lambert agreed. He saw no need to add that it had been sharpened very recently and the point ground down a little. "It's possible whoever killed Mr. Boston took it from Mr. Chester's kitchen. He said he didn't know if he had any like it, or if one was missing, and we should ask you."

"Nobody took that knife from there," Elsie answered very positively. "Mr. Chester's knives are dif'rent. Expensive."

"All of them?"

"Yes. There's not one like that in the 'ouse."

There was little more she could tell them. Clearly she liked Susan Wareham and had little use for Alethea Wightman or Carole Boston.

178

The Lanes were "all right, I s'pose," but didn't really belong to the village. Lambert and Flick stood up to go.

As Elsie opened the door for them, Lambert asked her, "Which way did you leave when you went home, Miss Hemmings?"

"The back door. Like I always do." Elsie sounded shocked at the suggestion she would take the liberty of using any other.

"The side door sticks, doesn't it?"

"Sometimes it does."

"At the top or the bottom?"

"The top. Mr. Chester keeps saying 'e'll do something about it, but 'e never does."

"Well, thank you for your help, Miss Hemmings," Lambert said. "One of my men will be coming to take a statement from you, but that's nothing for you to worry about."

"It won't worry me," Elsie replied with spirit, closing the door. Lambert and Flick got back into their car. Just along the road a few ducks were paddling rather aimlessly on the pond and a coot was making a great to-do as it tore across the water. Two small boys were exploring the banks of the River Frew where it was overhung by trees just upstream from the bridge. One of them had a home-made fishing-rod.

As soon as they rounded the bend by the gates of Frewley Priory Flick and Lambert saw the cars parked down the road and the small crowd gathered outside Forge Cottage. Lambert swore under his breath. It was inevitable that reporters would congregate after a murder when the victim was as well known as Boston, but still he disliked it; personally, because it seemed to him like a callous cashing in on other people's tragedies, and professionally because they were one more distraction when the job was already complicated and difficult enough without them. And while there were times when the press could help, and did so readily, he couldn't see this being one of them.

Flick was still wondering whether she should apologize for nearly laughing aloud back there at Elsie Hemmings' cottage. She was sure Lambert had seen through her nose blowing. Now, hearing him curse softly, she decided to hold her tongue.

"Do you know which house is the Lanes'?" he asked her, slowing the car almost to walking pace.

"The one next to the church, sir. The red brick one."

"Queen Anne."

"Yes, sir."

Lambert glanced sideways at her, but Flick was looking straight ahead. "Nice," he commented, turning back to look at the house. "What about the depraved Hastings?"

"His is about fifty yards farther on, sir. It's called Oriel Cottage."

The pale blue Rolls was still parked on the drive beside Forge Cottage. Hooting to warn a photographer who stepped into the road just in front of them, Lambert turned in and stopped behind it. At least, he told himself, the press didn't know him, and Flick in her summer dress and the unmarked car didn't exactly shout "Police."

Chester answered his ring so quickly Lambert wondered if he had been expecting somebody. This morning he was wearing a faded blue T-shirt with the name of his university emblazoned across it, equally shabby jeans and training shoes.

"Come in," he greeted them hospitably. "But I suppose you would anyway." Closing the door, he led the way to the drawing-room. "I take it you want to ask me some more questions."

"I'm afraid so," Lambert replied. "But first, I would like to have another quick look in your kitchen."

Chester looked amused. "By all means. Are you still looking for missing knives?"

He was taking all this pretty coolly, Lambert thought. Last evening was different, you had to allow for them all being keyed up, and people reacted to tension in different ways, but by now there had been time for the enormity of what had happened here in his house to come home to him. And he must realize the murderer was one of his guests.

As if he had read the other man's thoughts, Chester said apologetically, "I'm sorry if I sound flippant. Don't think I'm not shocked, it was an appalling thing to happen."

Lambert nodded and went out of the room. From where she was sitting Flick could see him turn into the kitchen and shut the door. What was he interested in there? she wondered. He had examined the kitchen thoroughly last night, together with the study and the hall, and Elsie Hemmings had assured them the knife hadn't come from there. She realized Chester was speaking to her.

"What's your superintendent's Christian name?" he asked.

"Neil," she replied, surprised. "But I shouldn't call him that if I were you."

"I won't," Chester assured her. "Is his second name Gordon?"

"Yes, it is. Why are you asking?"

Chester smiled. "Nothing for you to worry about. Honestly." Flick hoped she could believe him. It was very quiet in the big room. With the sun obscured by cloud today there were no shadows across the lawn and the garden furniture looked forlorn and neglected. Even the birds were silent. Then Lambert returned.

"All right?" Chester enquired.

"Yes, thank you." Lambert's face was expressionless. "Did you tell any of your guests who was going to be here yesterday?"

"No."

"Was there any special reason why you didn't?"

Chester hesitated for a second or two before answering, "No, not really."

"It wasn't because you knew most of the others couldn't stand Mr. Boston?"

"No. In any case, I wouldn't put it as strongly as that."

"Wouldn't you? They made no bones about it. Why did you ask those particular people, Mr. Chester?"

For the first time Chester looked mildly concerned. "The main object was for Miss Wightman to meet Mrs. Lane. I was pretty sure she was going to take Gillian's book, and I wanted to help in any way I could. I'd been going to ask Alethea down here for some time, I'd nothing on this weekend, and it fitted in well. It may seem old-fashioned to you, but I didn't think I could ask her without inviting another woman and I knew her firm had published Tommy Boston's autobiography. I had no idea she disliked him so much. To tell you the truth, when I found out I was a bit shaken, but it was too late to do anything about it then. I invited Hastings because we knew each other and I thought he'd have something in common with Alethea and Gillian."

"You knew he had ghosted Mr. Boston's book?"

"Not then. He told me yesterday evening."

Lambert wondered if that was true. If it was, Chester had been singularly unfortunate in his choice of guests. On the other hand, it all seemed plausible enough. And what reason could he have had for inviting people he knew detested Boston? Lambert could think of only one: if Chester had set out to provide a field of suspects in order that his own motive for killing the comedian, whatever it was, wouldn't be so noticeable. It seemed pretty far-fetched.

"I've been reading his book," he said.

"Oh?" Chester looked interested. "What's your verdict?"

"I thought it dull and irritatingly self-satisfied. The writing was flat." Lambert smiled. "But I'm not a critic."

"No, you aren't, are you?" Chester returned the smile. "But you're right, it was bloody flat. When I read it I thought that was just Tommy's not really being a writer—although I must say I was surprised he could write at all. Peter's much brighter than you might think, but he has no imagination. It's why his novels are so third-rate. He should have stuck to journalism. Not that you don't need imagination for that," Chester added cynically.

"As far as you know then," Lambert said, "none of them knew who else would be here?"

"Miss Wightman knew Mrs. Lane would and *vice versa*."

"But none of the others knew the Bostons were coming?"

"No."

"Not even Miss Wareham?"

Again there was the briefest of pauses before Chester replied. "Not until Friday afternoon," he said.

"Surely you told her before then? She's your secretary, and she was going to be here. After all, it wasn't a secret, was it?"

"No. I just didn't, there wasn't any special reason."

Lambert wondered if the other man was hiding something. But he didn't comment, and after a few seconds Chester went on in a different tone, sounding at ease and cheerful again, "You know, in a terrible way this business is like a golden-age detective story: the party, the body in the study—not quite a library, I grant you, but as near as you can expect to get these days—a victim disliked by pretty well everybody, a locked room, and a detective who writes mystery stories." He stopped and regarded Lambert with an expression of quizzical amusement.

"Oh?" Lambert queried politely. He knew Chester was trying to side-track him, and knowing was half the battle.

"Only he's not the brilliant amateur as he would be in a book, he's the policeman. I am right, aren't I?"

Flick looked from one man to the other and wondered uneasily if this was why Chester had wanted to know the super's Christian names. She hoped she hadn't done wrong telling him.

"How did you find out?" Lambert asked coolly.

"Does it matter?"

"No." He didn't care much. It was irritating, Chester's knowing, but that was all. "I keep my job and my writing quite separate," he said.

"Do you?" Chester's bushy eyebrows rose and he smiled a shade sardonically. "You know, I'm sorry, but I find that very hard to believe. You may honestly think you do, but in practice it's impossible. You use things you see and hear as a policeman, and people you meet, consciously or unconsciously in your books. You can't help it."

Lambert, who had been about to admit as much, changed his mind and said instead, "That has nothing to do with the reason for our being here now." As far as Chester and the rest of his party were concerned he should be a cipher. He could, within certain constraints, be understanding, even compassionate, but that mustn't affect the way he did his job. He must remain a figure without discernible likes and dislikes, without a personality, prejudices or feelings. To them he must be a functionary, no more and no less. It was one of the things about his work Barbara had hated.

Now Chester was trying to put flesh on the bones and to remind him that he was a human being with a life outside his job. With his own vulnerabilities. What was worse, he was trying to fit him into some crack-brained idea of his own. What motive could he have, apart from showing off that he knew he, Lambert, was Neil Laming, the author of eight moderately successful mystery novels and half a dozen short stories? But showing off his knowledge, however trivial it might be, was probably always sufficient motive for Chester. And surely it couldn't be a subtle form of blackmail.

"Will you come on my programme when all this is over?" Chester asked cheerfully.

"No, I won't." Lambert didn't know whether to be very angry or only amused.

Chester looked contrite. "I'm sorry, that was the wrong thing to say, wasn't it? Forget it." He paused. "Tommy Boston was killed between two thirty-two and three o'clock, right?"

"It seems likely," Lambert agreed.

"He must have been, he wasn't in the study when I looked in there at two thirty-two, and the door was locked when Carole went to find him at three. I grant you it isn't a hundred per cent proved, he could have been alive in there with whoever murdered him, but it hardly seems likely. And I should think Susan and I would have heard something if he was killed while we were in the kitchen. So it was most probably after we took the drinks out to the others at two forty-five. That means we can eliminate everybody who has an alibi for those twenty-eight minutes: Gillian Lane, Carole Boston, Hastings, Susan and me. Am I right so far?"

Chester's breezy manner was grating on Lambert as much as his apparent assumption that they were partners in the investigation. He remembered what Beeley had said about the whole case being too much like a detective story. Now Chester was saying the same thing, and, worse, he was behaving as if he were the detective in it showing the bumbling policeman the line he should pursue. Did it mean so little to him a cold-blooded murder had been committed here in his house less than twenty-four hours ago? Either he was extraordinarily insensitive or there was a reason for his behaviour.

"You were alone in the kitchen for eight minutes before Miss Wareham got back," he said coolly. "You had as much opportunity as anybody to kill Tommy Boston."

11

FOR a moment they stared at each other in silence. Then, "I wondered when you'd get round to that," Chester said. "I can't expect you to take my word that I didn't do it."

"And so far we've no confirmation of Miss Wareham's account of her movements between two-fifteen and two-forty," Lambert continued as if Chester hadn't spoken.

"You can't think she had anything to do with it," Chester protested. "She wouldn't hurt anybody, let alone plan a cold-blooded murder. And what possible motive could she have had? She hadn't met Boston before yesterday."

There was something false about the man's seemingly relaxed manner, Lambert thought. This last exchange mattered more to him than he wanted them to see.

"We're looking into everybody's possible motives," he said.

"I'm sure you are." Chester waited a moment, and when Lambert said nothing, went on, "You agree that the most important factor in this whole business is the locked room?"

"Perhaps."

"If you eliminate those five—Mrs. Lane, Peter Hastings, Susan Wareham, Mrs. Boston and me—you're left with two people, Miss Wightman and Trevor Lane. Alethea Wightman says she was in her room all the time, but nobody saw her and she can't prove it. And Bert Jarman at the Wheatsheaf says Trevor left there at a quarter to three."

Lambert didn't like this; Chester, it seemed, was making his own enquiries. But unless he interfered with witnesses or hampered the police in some other way, there was little they could do about it.

"I went across to the post office for my papers before breakfast," Chester was saying. "Just inside the door there's a display of kitchen knives. Two of them are missing."

"You're suggesting somebody in your party went across and bought or stole one of them?" Lambert asked.

"Not suggesting, just considering it as a possibility."

"Miss Wareham says she was in the post office shortly before Boston was killed."

192

"I told you, I'm certain she had nothing to do with it," Chester said forcefully.

Lambert let it go. "I understand Mr. Boston didn't behave very well at lunch," he said, "suggesting he'd written books he almost certainly hadn't, annoying Mrs. Lane and taunting Mr. Hastings."

"So you've heard about that."

"Yes. You didn't mention it, didn't you want us to know?"

"It was irrelevant." Chester brushed the question aside.

"It's too early yet to say what's relevant and what isn't," Lambert retorted. "We're still collecting facts—and we need to know everything that happened."

"Yes, of course. I'm sorry." Chester hardly sounded contrite.

"You said the key was in the lock on the inside of the study door when you climbed in," Lambert reminded him. "That's right, isn't it?"

"Yes. That was the whole point, surely?" Chester replied.

"It seems like it," Lambert conceded. Apparently he was satisfied, for he changed the subject. "You know of no reason why anybody who was here yesterday should have wanted to kill Mr. Boston?"

"No. Some of them may have disliked him, but you don't kill people just because you don't like them."

"Normal people don't. Not just for that."

Chester regarded Lambert quizzically. "I don't know of anything else," he said.

Lambert took the photograph of the knife from its envelope. "Are you sure you don't recognize this knife?" he asked.

Chester studied the picture and handed it back. "Not specifically," he said. "I mean, it's just an ordinary kitchen knife, isn't it? There must be millions of them about. As far as I know, I haven't one like it, if that's what you mean."

That confirmed what Elsie Hemmings had told them, and what he had discovered when he examined the kitchen yesterday evening, Lambert told himself. Not that it was conclusive, there could have been an odd knife lying about, in the tool shed perhaps, of which Elsie knew nothing. Or Chester could have bought it some time ago and hidden it away, ready to be used when the opportunity arose.

"There's nothing else you can tell us?" he asked.

Chester's eyes met his innocently and he shook his head. "No," he replied. "If I think of anything, I'll get in touch with you straightaway."

Lambert nodded. "Yes, thank you," he said. "That's all for the time being, Mr. Chester. Except that I'd like to have a quick look in your study, please."

"Yes, of course," Chester agreed.

Flick put her notebook and ball-point away in her bag and stood up. Why did the super want to have another look in the study? she wondered.

Chester must have had the same thought; he watched curiously as Lambert walked across to the nearest set of bookshelves. "There are two of yours there," he remarked.

"So I noticed yesterday," Lambert told him, rejoining him and Flick in the hall. "They weren't what I was looking for. I see you have quite a collection of John Dickson Carr's books."

"Oh, so that's it." Chester smiled. "Of course I have, he was a major figure in the history of crime fiction."

"I wonder if there's a parallel to this case in any of his books."

"I've no idea."

Chester was still smiling. It was a rather complacent smile, Flick thought. She didn't like it, and she wondered what this talk about some author she'd never heard of meant.

Lambert walked to the side door and opened it. It stuck slightly at the top. "Goodbye, Mr. Chester," he said.

"Goodbye, Superintendent. Goodbye, Miss Graham. If your boss won't come on my programme, perhaps you will," Chester said incorrigibly.

He stood in the doorway watching while they got into their car and reversed out into the road.

"Well, what did you make of all that?" Lambert asked Flick as they drove through the village.

"He's too clever by half," she answered.

"He is, isn't he? But I think all that talk was a smoke-screen to hide something, his real feelings, or guilt—or just knowledge he didn't want us to know he possessed. Under the bright chat he was tense. Especially when we were talking about Susan Wareham."

"He was very insistent the murder must have

been committed between two thirty-two and three, yet he hasn't an alibi for part of the time," Flick remarked. "Isn't that odd for somebody who thinks such a lot of himself?"

"It could be he gets a kick out of being a suspect," Lambert said. "I got the impression he was telling us a story he knew had a weakness in it—trying it on for size, to see if we'd spot that weakness." He stopped, then went on, "It was interesting what he said about Hastings having no imagination; this affair has all the hallmarks of a murderer with a lot."

"Hastings couldn't have done it anyway, could he?" Flick said.

"On the face of it none of them could except Miss Wightman and Lane—and possibly Chester. So he wasn't changing anything by giving us another reason why Hastings could be ruled out. It was a perfectly valid point, anyhow."

"Sir," Flick ventured, "what was all that about John Dickson Carr?"

Lambert smiled. "Oh, he was a famous detective-story writer, the king of the locked-room puzzle. Most of the murders in his books seemed as if they couldn't have been committed because the room was sealed on the inside or there were only the victim's footprints in the wet sand."

"Oh," Flick said.

Lambert slowed the car. "I've forgotten something. We'll have to go back."

"To Logan Chester's?" Flick asked.

"No, the Lanes'."

They had just passed a farm entrance on the left. Lambert reversed into it and drove back towards the village.

"I shan't go to church today," Cicely Robins said. "People would stare so. I shouldn't mind that very much, but it would make it difficult to concentrate, and I have to concentrate so hard nowadays, or I just mouth things without thinking what I'm saying."

Gillian smiled affectionately at her mother. "Going to church means a lot to you, doesn't it?" she asked.

"Yes, dear, it does. When I was a little girl we went at least once every Sunday, and for a long time it was just habit. I hardly thought about what I was doing there. Now, the older I get the more important it becomes. Do you think that's devoutness or cowardice?"

Gillian laughed. "I'm sure it's not cowardice in your case," she replied.

"I do wonder sometimes. I meant to ask you, but I forgot with that dreadful murder and everything," Cicely said. "What was Miss Wightman like?"

Gillian thought. "I don't know really; we didn't have a chance to have a proper talk. She seemed terribly vague, but Logan says she's very good at her job, and she was quite nice to me. Only I thought she was a terrible snob, and I can't stand snobs."

"That's because people like us don't need to be snobbish," her mother told her. "Snobbishness is so vulgar."

Gillian stared in amazement. "That," she declared, "is the most snobbish thing I've ever heard."

"Yes, dear, I suppose it is," Cicely agreed complacently. She laughed. "How long is Mrs. Boston staying?"

"Only today."

"Poor girl. It must be terribly depressing to have your husband murdered, even if you did sometimes wish he were dead."

"You think Carole . . . ?" Gillian asked,

horrified. Really, her mother did say the most extraordinary things.

"Wished he was out of the way? Oh yes, I expect so. Most wives do. Not necessarily dead, perhaps, but that's so much more certain; people who are dead can't make trouble later. Well, they can with their wills and things, of course—but you know what I mean. And divorce can be so demoralizing," Cicely added, giving her daughter a sidelong look. "You say she's quite a nice girl really, and from what you've told me about Mr. Boston, she must have done. Quite often, I should think. But wishing something and having it come true are quite different. At least . . ."

"At least what?" Gillian demanded. She was disturbed. Surely her mother couldn't think Carole had stabbed Tommy Boston. But hadn't she wondered herself?

Cicely smiled sweetly. "Nothing, dear. I was just thinking aloud. Now I *must* go and see to those dead roses. I intended to do them yesterday, but it was so hot and I was rather tired. It's stopped raining now, too."

As she went out of the room the front door-bell rang and Gillian went to answer it. Lambert and Flick were on the doorstep.

"Oh, it's you," she said, not meaning it rudely.

"May we come in?" Lambert asked. "There are a lot of reporters just down the road; they'll have seen our car."

"They've already been here," Gillian told him resignedly. "But you'd better come in."

She led the way into a large, high-ceilinged drawing-room at the front of the house. Lambert thought that when he was a small boy the drawing-room at his home had hardly been used except on Sundays, and how when, a young and diffident constable, he had first entered a room like this he had had an odd sensation that he was both large and clumsy and very small at the same time. The room had belonged to a sharp-tongued old lady and there were several large and, he feared, valuable vases standing on the floor and on small tables. He had been worried he would knock one over and break it.

"Have we got to answer *more* questions?" Gillian asked wearily. She didn't sit down herself or suggest they should.

"Not exactly," Lambert told her cheerfully. "The main reason for our coming to see you is to ask if I could borrow a copy of your novel."

Gillian looked surprised. "Why do you want it?" she asked. "It hasn't been published yet, and you can't want to read it; I wouldn't think it's your kind of book at all." Realizing that might have sounded rude, she blushed faintly.

"We have to do all sorts of things in the line of duty," Lambert told her ironically.

"I'm sorry, I didn't mean . . . What I meant was, it's the sort of book that's more likely to appeal to women than men," Gillian said.

"You have a copy of the typescript?" Lambert asked her.

"Yes. Yes, I have. But I don't see why . . . It hasn't anything to do with—with what happened yesterday. It can't have."

"I don't suppose it has for a moment." Lambert's tone was reassuring. "We'll take good care of it. If you wouldn't mind?"

"Very well."

"And perhaps we could have a quick word with Mr. Lane while you're fetching it."

"I'll tell him," Gillian said.

She went out of the room, looking unhappy. There were two books on the table beside Lambert and he picked them up. One was a thriller by Dick Francis, the other a reprint of an old detective story by Carter Dickson.

Lambert studied it with interest, flipping through the pages and reading passages here and there. "It could be coincidence," he murmured.

"Sir?" Flick said.

"Carter Dickson was a pen-name of John Dickson Carr's," Lambert told her. "This book's due back tomorrow, so whoever borrowed it from the library must have taken it out three weeks ago.

He put it down on the table and a moment later Trevor Lane walked in. "You want to see me?" he demanded shortly.

"There are just two or three points, Mr. Lane," Lambert said. "First, you said you got back from the Wheatsheaf just as Mr. Chester was going into the house to find Mr. Boston. Is that right?" Trevor nodded. "That was just after three o'clock."

"If you say so."

"Mr. Chester is sure it was. The last customers left the Wheatsheaf at two forty-five. It takes about a minute to walk from there to Forge Cottage. What were you doing for that quarter of an hour, Mr. Lane?"

The silence in the big room was almost tangible, Flick thought. She could feel the tension. A car drove past, slowed for the bend and accelerated away again. The sound of its engine faded into the distance.

"I went and sat in my car," Trevor said at last.

"Oh?" Lambert's tone was noncommittal, yet somehow it implied scepticism. "For the whole fifteen minutes?"

"Is there any law against it?" Trevor demanded. Lambert didn't answer, and after a moment he muttered, "There was something I wanted to think about."

"Your argument with your wife?" Lambert suggested.

"Did she tell you about it?"

"Or was it how you were going to kill Tommy Boston?"

"No!" Trevor almost shouted. Lambert waited. "Blast you! It was about my wife and me."

"When you went to the pub you went out by the side door, right?" Lambert said. Trevor nodded. He was still angry and resentful. "Did you come back the same way?"

"Yes."

"Did you notice the door stick either time?" Lambert asked.

The question seemed to surprise Trevor and he relaxed slightly. "Not that I remember," he answered. "Wait a minute, it did a bit."

"You're sure?"

"Yes. It wasn't much, though, I just had to pull it a bit harder."

"Can you remember if it stuck at the top or the bottom?"

"The top. What's all this about?"

"Nothing very much."

The door opened and Gillian came in carrying a bulky envelope file. With an anxious glance at her husband, she perched on the arm of an easy chair.

"One other thing, Mr. Lane," Lambert said. "Will you tell me exactly what happened when you and Mr. Chester went to find Mr. Boston?"

"I've told you already," Trevor protested.

"I know you have, but I want to be certain I have every detail clear."

Resignedly Trevor repeated his account. Lambert let him tell it without interruptions until he came to the point where they had seen Boston lying on the floor through the study window. Then he asked, "Mr. Chester sent Mr. Hastings to ring the doctor before he climbed in?"

"Yes," Trevor replied.

"Where was he when he asked you to go back to the hall and he'd unlock the study door to let you in?"

"Just going to climb in." Trevor glanced at Gillian. "It took him some time, it was all he could do to hoist himself up. I waited to see he'd got in all right, then I went. When he let me in I asked him how Boston was, but he said he hadn't looked at him yet."

"Where was he when you left him?" Lambert asked.

"Walking across to the door."

"And the key was in the lock?"

"Yes."

Lambert paused. "Could you see if there was a paper-knife on the desk?" he asked.

Trevor looked startled. "Paper-knife?" he repeated. "But it was a kitchen knife that—" He stopped. "I couldn't see, the sun was on the other side of the house and it was pretty dim in there."

Lambert nodded. "Thank you, Mr. Lane. That was very clear." He produced the photograph he had shown Elsie Hemmings and Chester. "Do either of you recognize this knife by any chance?"

Gillian stared, horrified, at the picture. "Is that the one?" she asked.

"Yes," Lambert told her.

"It looks like an ordinary kitchen knife," Trevor said. "We've got several of them."

"Mrs. Lane?"

"Yes," Gillian muttered.

"I wonder if you'd be good enough to go with WPC Graham here to make sure none of them are missing." Lambert asked. "It's just routine; there's a possibility this one was stolen."

He didn't expect them to take his words at their face value; they were intelligent enough to know why he was checking. If they had a set similar to the murder weapon, and that size was missing, it would be another fact to be noted. Possibly significant, just as likely not. Plenty of kitchens had collections of odd knives rather than matching sets.

Anyway, Gillian couldn't have killed Boston, Lambert thought, as she went out without a word, Flick at her heels. Casually he picked up the library books from the table and looked at them.

"Does Mrs. Lane read detective stories?" he asked.

"They're mine," Trevor answered. "I read

thrillers sometimes. They're the only sort of books I can be bothered with."

"You've read these?"

"Yes."

Lambert knew Carter Dickson's novel was about a murder in a locked room, but Trevor showed no sign of remembering it. Had he already forgotten, or did he hope Lambert knew nothing about the book? Certainly he seemed restless and uneasy.

It was several minutes before Gillian and Flick returned and they passed slowly and in silence. When they came in Flick looked at Lambert and shook her head almost imperceptibly.

Gillian picked up the file from the table where she had put it when she left the room. "The typescript's in there," she said, handing it to Lambert. "It's the only copy I've got; will I get it back?"

"Unless it's wanted for evidence, and I don't see why it should be," Lambert replied. "Thank you."

"That's all?" Trevor asked.

"For now, yes."

Trevor saw Lambert and Flick out.

"Interesting," Lambert remarked as they

drove away. In his rear-view mirror he could see the reporters still clustered in a group outside Forge Cottage.

"What Lane said, you mean, sir?" Flick enquired.

"That and other things. Mrs. Lane's worried sick he killed Boston, you can see that. I'd say he has a nasty temper and Boston got right under his skin at lunch, making out he'd read her book when Lane hadn't, and trying to play games with her under the table."

"But he wouldn't kill him for that," Mick protested.

"Men have been murdered for a lot less. And Lane's probably the jealous type. If he'd already drunk a good deal before he went back to the pub after lunch, and then went to have it out with Boston . . ."

Was that what Lane had really been doing, sitting out there in his car? Bringing himself to the pitch of carrying out his plan to murder Boston? Always granted, of course, that he had been telling the truth about where he'd spent that quarter of an hour. If the knife hadn't come from Forge Cottage, the murderer must either have brought it with him—or her—or acquired it after he arrived. Chester had said there were similar knives on display in the post office, could the killer have slipped in there when the shop was busy, purloined one of them and slipped out again unnoticed? Perhaps on the way to or from the pub before lunch, or, more likely, afterwards? If so, he must have known they were there. Roger Beeley was checking at the post office, he might be able to say more about that.

"You didn't find anything in the kitchen then?" Lambert asked. "From the time you were gone I imagined there was something."

"There was a set of knives on a board on the wall, sir," Flick replied rather stiffly. Her pride was hurt. After all, there was a good reason for her being so long. "They were a different sort, expensive ones like Logan Chester's, and they were all there. There were some odd ones in a drawer. Mrs. Lane said there were none missing, but she could have been lying."

"You think she was?"

"No, I think it was the truth. I was rather a long time because she said I'd better look in her mother's kitchen, too, while I was about it. She was being sarcastic, but I thought I should."

"Her mother?" Lambert queried. It was the first he had heard of Gillian Lane's mother living in the house.

"Yes, sir. She has a granny flat." Flick, who could never remain on her dignity for long, grinned. "She's a nice old thing. She insisted I look in all the drawers and cupboards. There were several knives, but she was positive none were missing."

Lambert grunted. He hadn't expected they would succeed in tracing the knife which killed Boston, and it looked as if he was going to be proved right.

"Aren't we forgetting something, sir?" Flick asked diffidently.

"What's that?"

"What Elsie Hemmings said about seeing Carole Boston coming out of Hastings' cottage."

"I hadn't forgotten," Lambert told her. "If they were having it off, it could give one of them a motive, I suppose, and Hastings hated Boston, but he can't have killed him, he was on the lawn with the others from before two-thirty until the body was found."

"I didn't think about that," Flick admitted.

She looked so crestfallen Lambert laughed. However, it took a good deal to keep her down-hearted for long.

"Why do you think Logan Chester's so keen to

make it all seem like a mystery story, sir?" she asked.

"The murderer did that," Lambert answered. "Not Chester—unless he is the murderer. He's just pointing out the similarities that are already there. And he's shielding somebody. From the way he got so tense when we were talking about her, I'd say it's Miss Wareham. What did you think of her?"

"Career girl who's got it bad for her boss," Flick replied without hesitation. "Intelligent, generous, and probably brave if she has to be. I can't see her killing Boston."

"You think she's in love with Chester?" Lambert asked. "Is that feminine intuition, or did she say something when you were out there on the lawn with them?"

"Neither, sir. Observation and deduction," Flick told him.

"If she is . . ." Lambert paused. "You know what happens in nearly every detective story, don't you?"

Flick shook her head.

"There's a second murder," Lambert told her.

12

"MISS WAREHAM phoned, sir," a uniformed sergeant informed him when, twenty minutes later, he and Flick entered the room allocated to the murder team.

"What did she want?" Lambert asked. Susan Wareham hadn't struck him as the sort of woman to indulge in flights of fancy or call the police on the slightest pretext.

"You, sir," the sergeant replied. "She wouldn't say what it was about, just that she'd remembered something. She left a number, and said she'd be there the rest of the morning." He handed Lambert a sheet torn from an official memo pad.

"Anything else?"

"No, sir."

"Nothing yet from Dr. Hewlett or the forensic people?"

"Not yet."

Lambert took the paper into his room and sat down at his desk. He didn't like this case.

In any investigation you had to sift the facts which were relevant from those which weren't, but this one had too many elaborations. He still didn't know why the murderer had arranged the locked room.

On a day like yesterday, surely at least one of the study windows would have been left open. Yet when Chester and Lane went to look they were both shut fast. Why had the killer, with Boston's body there on the floor, taken time to secure them and lock the door on the inside? As Beeley had pointed out, most people would have left the room as quickly as possible.

Three people could have murdered the comedian: Alethea Wightman, Lane and Chester. Plus, just possibly, Susan Wareham. Which of them possessed the sort of imagination as well as the nerve and ruthlessness this crime had required? Lambert didn't doubt that Alethea had the brains, and she had been alone in the house for the whole of the crucial twenty-five minutes. She probably had the nerve and the ruthless streak, too, but where was her motive? Could Boston have been blackmailing her? From what he had heard of the dead man, Lambert wouldn't put a little blackmail past him. So far there was no evidence, but perhaps he would learn something when he started delving into Alethea's background.

Trevor Lane might possess the nerve and a motive, although they hadn't unearthed a convincing one yet; Lambert doubted if he had the imagination. He was by no means a fool, but his intelligence was of a different kind. His wife was another matter, and there was probably a steely streak behind those lovely features. Lane had said the books on the table in their house were his, but she could have read them. And whether she had or not, they could have planned the murder together. Was that what they had really been talking about in the garden after lunch, not her novel? It would account for Trevor's being on edge, and his wife's anxiety although she had an alibi. The difficulty there was that the murder must have been planned in advance while, as far as was known, neither of the Lanes had ever met Boston until yesterday.

Chester was exactly as he appeared on television, conceited, clever, self-assured. He enjoyed showing off and manipulating people; look how he had tried to dictate the way the investigation should be run. He seemed to believe quite genuinely that he was cleverer than other people—and that was dangerous.

Chester had had opportunity, and you couldn't get away from the fact that it was his party. Why, unless it was to act as a smoke-screen for what he planned, had he brought together a group of people he might have known wouldn't mix amicably, to put it mildly? But where was his motive? If he was right, Lambert thought, and Chester was shielding somebody, almost certainly it wasn't Alethea Wightman.

Susan Wareham, too, might possess both brains and nerve, and, according to Lane, the side door had stuck only slightly when he returned to the house just after three. She could have re-entered it that way, killed Boston, and gone out again, before walking round to the kitchen. She knew the door stuck sometimes better than anyone except Chester.

Earlier that morning Lambert had had the glimmerings of an idea. It hadn't taken shape and now, hunched over his desk, he tried to recapture it. Without success, it remained nebulous, just beyond his grasp.

The telephone rang. Swearing softly, he lifted the receiver.

"Lambert."

"Dr. Hewlett for you, sir," the woman on the switchboard told him.

"Put him through," he said.

"Superintendent Lambert?" The pathologist's thin, slightly high-pitched tones were unmistakable.

"Yes, Doctor?"

"I haven't written my report yet, of course," Hewlett said, "but I thought you'd like an idea of what will be in it."

"That's very good of you.".

"I'll spare you the fancy stuff. Your man was killed by a single stab wound in the heart inflicted with a knife with a blade approximately an inch wide and at least five inches long. Almost certainly the one you found in the body."

Lambert told himself to be patient, Hewlett wouldn't have rung to tell him only what he already knew.

"There were traces of soil in the wound," the pathologist continued.

"Soil?" He had all Lambert's attention now.

"That's right. The stuff I'd be working on in my garden now if it wasn't for you and your unfortunate corpse. I'd say it was on the knife when they stuck it in him. There was only a very small amount, but I've probably recovered enough for your people to make something of it."

"Thank you," Lambert said. Soil! he thought.

"Don't mention it, Superintendent. That's what the government pays my munificent fees for."

Sarcastic old fool, Lambert thought. He didn't mean it, he knew Hewlett was anything but a fool.

"You want to know when he died?" the pathologist asked.

"It would help."

"I thought it might. Not less than twenty minutes after his last meal and not more than forty. He had salmon and a rather nice piece of Stilton, by the way."

"That ties in," Lambert said incautiously. He supposed pathologists had to possess that kind of sense of humour to retain their sanity.

"It had better, there's no doubt about it," Hewlett commented tartly. "Ironic somebody may get life for killing him, he'd have gone in the next year without their help, the mess he was in. If you're interested, I'd say the probability is your murderer's righthanded, but I wouldn't stand up in court and swear to it. That's about all I can tell you."

"I'm very grateful, Doctor," Lambert said.

"A pleasure, my boy. This is your first murder on your own, isn't it? The best of luck to you."

"Thank you." Lambert was astounded Hewlett had remembered.

Forty minutes after two-ten was two-fifty, he thought when he had replaced the phone. Say a minute or two either way to allow for Susan Wareham's not being exact. As he had said, that fitted the evidence they already had that the murder must have been committed between two thirty-two and three. The presence of soil in the wound was interesting, but unless the people at the forensic science laboratory said it hadn't come from the garden at Forge Cottage and where it had, he couldn't see it took them any farther. Nothing seemed to, he thought gloomily. And yet, just before Hewlett rang he had believed he was on to something. What was it? But the memory still eluded him.

The telephone rang again. This time it was the assistant chief constable wanting to know what progress was being made and what

Lambert thought should go into the statement for the press.

"We must give them something," he lamented in his mournful voice. "A case like this . . ."

Lambert knew he was right, and he read out the draft he had already prepared. He suspected that if John Firbank, the head of the county CID, hadn't been on leave somewhere in Cornwall and his deputy too involved in a big drugs case to be taken off it, one of them would have been put in charge of the investigation. The assistant chief constable was a past master at promoting the belief everything possible was being done, whether the matter at issue was manning a school crossing or a major crime.

"It's our function to serve the public, and we must show them we're doing it," was his favourite maxim. Even if it was a lot of bull and precious little else, some of his subordinates were inclined to comment behind his back.

"Yes, good. That seems to fit the bill," he agreed now, his relief clear over the telephone. "I'll leave it to you then, Neil. Keep me in the picture."

"Yes, sir," Lambert said. At least they both wanted the same thing, he thought: to keep the press off their backs. He put the phone down, then picked it up again and dialled the number on the sheet of paper the sergeant had given him.

"Hallo?" He recognized Susan's voice immediately.

"Miss Wareham? Superintendent Lambert. I understand you rang while I was out."

"Yes. I've remembered something. I don't suppose it's at all important, but you said let you know if there was anything."

"That's right," Lambert agreed. "I'm afraid there are a few more questions I have to ask you now we know a little more. I was coming to see you this afternoon. Would three-thirty suit you?"

Susan hesitated. It would mean ringing Nina to say she wouldn't be able to look after Simon today, but surely this once wouldn't matter. She was reluctant to tell Lambert this afternoon wouldn't be convenient; he might wonder why not. "Yes," she said, "that'll be all right. You know where I live?" Of course he did, she told herself, the police had taken all their addresses yesterday. "How to find it, I mean?"

"Yes, thank you," Lambert told her.

Susan had just put down the phone when it rang again. This time it was Chester.

"Are you all right?" he asked.

"Yes, of course." It was unlike him to be so solicitous and she felt a little glow of pleasure. "I'm in a bit of a state of shock, but I suppose we all are."

"Yes," Chester agreed. "What are you doing today?"

"Nothing much. The superintendent's coming this afternoon; he says there are some more questions he has to ask me. And I've remembered something." The words had come out without her thinking about them, she hadn't been going to mention that to Logan. But it seemed disloyal somehow to tell Lambert behind his back.

"What's that?" he enquired.

"Only that my watch was five minutes slow yesterday. It had stopped, and when I put it on again I got it wrong. It was a quarter to three when I got back from Miss Rider's, not twenty to. I know it doesn't matter, but I thought I should tell him."

There was a moment's silence before Chester said, "Yes. Look, don't worry, Sue. Just keep your head and everything will be all right."

"Like Kipling," Susan said idiotically. She felt a little lightheaded.

"Kipling?" Chester said, sounding puzzled.

"You know, 'If you can keep your head when all about are losing theirs . . .'"

"Oh that. Yes. Would you like me to come over?"

Susan was more surprised than ever. It was very nice of him, but she really didn't need moral support just answering a few questions. "You?" she said. "What for?"

"I just thought . . ."

Oh dear, I've hurt him, Susan thought. "It's lovely of you to offer," she said, "but I'll be all right. Honestly."

"If you're sure. When's he coming?"

"Three-thirty. Why?"

"Nothing." Chester hesitated. "What about going out somewhere for dinner this evening?"

"Oh, I'd love to," Susan told him. During the months she had worked for him, Chester had taken her out to dinner twice, both times when he had kept her working late. Now, on the first occasion he asked her without feeling he was obliged to, he had to choose a time like this, she thought. She felt like laughing, but suspected that if she did, she would sound hysterical, and, anyway, he might think she was laughing at him. "Do you think we should?" she asked, doubts suddenly assailing her.

"Why not?"

"Well, I mean, it doesn't seem very appropriate somehow."

"Because a particularly unpleasant little man got himself murdered?" Chester asked. "It'll do us good to forget it all for an hour or two. Why should anyone else care?"

"All right, let's," Susan agreed. He was right, she supposed, but she wished he hadn't phrased it quite so coldly. Almost callously. Still, the prospect of spending the evening here on her own was depressing, and there couldn't be anything wrong in their having a quiet meal together, could there?

"I'll come for you at seven," Chester said.

"Great," she told him. Where would he take her? she wondered. What should she wear?

"And remember, Sue, as long as we stick together and keep our cool, everything will be all right."

"Yes, of course," Susan said, wondering what on earth he meant.

"'Bye."

"'Bye, Logan."

224

She replaced the phone in a daze. Underlying her joy at his taking the trouble to ring, and his asking her out, there was fear. Twice he had said something about their having to stick together, was he making a veiled call for her support? But how could she support him?

And surely, if he needed her backing, it could only be because . . . Oh God! she thought.

The telephone was on a small table by the window, and as she put it down she looked out. The street was almost deserted at this time on a Sunday and there was only one person in sight, a tall woman with her hair in a bun wearing a light coat which drooped from her thin shoulders. What on earth was Alethea Wightman doing here? Susan wondered.

Peter Hastings had to make an effort to walk across the green to the Wheatsheaf as usual that Sunday. He guessed that people would stare at him because he had "been there" yesterday. That didn't worry him so much, but the press would almost certainly be there, too, and he didn't want them asking him questions.

His fears were misplaced. After a few curious glances when he first came in, nobody seemed to be taking any notice of him. The Wheatsheaf was a popular pub, and at weekends it drew customers from miles around who didn't know him and were concerned with their own affairs. They and the reporters, a tight little group at the end of the bar, far outnumbered the local people, most of whom probably couldn't see him through the crowd, anyhow.

He was waiting to be served with his second pint when he overheard an old man sitting at a table beside him say, "It's terrible them stopping the buses on Sundays. My wife should be going to Wittenham to see her sister this afternoon. The old girl's nearly ninety and we had a call from the home yesterday to say she wasn't too good, and could one of us go? How can we? There's no bus except Tuesdays, Wednesdays and Fridays, and I gave up driving more than two years ago."

"I remember you did," his companion agreed.

"It'd cost a fortune to have a taxi there and back," the old man went on. He sighed. "I don't know."

George Layton was nearly eighty himself, and he had been coming to the Wheatsheaf for over fifty years. In the old days he had enjoyed his two pints of bitter; now he was reduced to a single bottle of light ale which he made last as long.

Hastings leaned over. "I couldn't help hearing what you were saying, Mr. Layton," he said. "Would it help if I ran Mrs. Layton over to Wittenham?"

The old man's expression brightened, but he was too proud and too diffident to accept at once. "It's very kind of you," he said uncertainly. "Are you sure it wouldn't be any trouble?"

"Positive," Hastings assured him.

"Then thank you very much indeed. It would be a great weight off our minds. My wife will be very grateful."

Hastings felt like saying he didn't want their gratitude. "Would a quarter past two suit her?" he asked.

"Yes. Yes, I'm sure it would," George Layton replied.

"I'll be at your house then," Hastings promised. He decided not to have a second pint after all and walked back across the green to find himself something for his lunch. He was glad he had offered to take Mrs. Layton, it made him feel good.

He and Carole had agreed it would be better

for them not to see each other for the next few days. There were too many prying eyes in the village, and if the reporters should see them together, they might start asking questions.

13

LUNCH at Bridge House was eaten in a strained atmosphere. Carole was still there, and Gillian had asked her mother to join them, but not even Cicely's well-intentioned chatter could relieve the uneasy gloom.

To add to Gillian's troubles Trevor had hardly spoken to her all morning. A few days ago she wouldn't have minded that, further evidence of his boorishness, it would have helped salve her conscience. Now she minded very much, and she felt helpless and hurt. That was bad enough; worse was the suspicion that, however hard he tried to conceal it, Trevor was afraid. Gillian had seen her mother eyeing him curiously once or twice. She's seen it, too, she thought.

Last night when she said, "You knew Tommy Boston before, didn't you?" she had wanted him to deny it and allay the fear which was tormenting her. Instead he had answered, "How did you know?" and she was shocked and frightened.

He had refused to tell her anything more, saying he didn't want to bother her with it. Didn't he see she was far more bothered not knowing?

"Are you doing anything this afternoon, Trevor?" she asked, passing him a bowl of strawberries.

"I thought I was taking Carole home," he said, looking at the girl who was sitting on his left. "Aren't I?"

That was why he had decided not to play cricket, Gillian thought. They had arranged it between them. Well, why shouldn't they? It was silly of her to mind.

"What's happening about your car, Carole?" she asked.

"I don't know," Carole replied. "Logan says I can leave it there for a day or two. I suppose I'll sell it sometime. I don't want it, it isn't my sort of car, and I always feel self-conscious in it." Carole paused. "The police want to search our house."

"They've been here," Gillian told her. She couldn't bring herself to say they were trying to trace the knife the murderer had used. "I expect they're looking in everybody's," she said.

"But there isn't anything there," Carole protested.

"It's routine," Trevor told her. "They'll want to look at Tommy's papers and that, to see if there's anything that'll give them a lead."

"I don't think he kept many papers."

"I shouldn't worry about it," Cicely said reassuringly. "Trevor's right, you know; I'm sure it is just routine. If you're innocent, you have nothing to fear. I always find that so comforting."

Gillian was gazing at her mother in horror.

"I can't help worrying," Carole said.

"No, of course you can't," Cicely agreed. Poor child, she thought. She can't have killed her husband, can she? But who could tell what went on behind those big blue eyes and pretty features? It was extraordinary to be sitting here, eating lunch and talking quite normally with someone who might be a murderess.

Gill, of course, was worried sick Trevor had killed that man. Perhaps that was no bad thing. That she was worried, she meant; it would show her how much she really cared for him.

Who was that clever old maid who solved the most baffling murders by finding parallels with incidents in the sleepy little village where she lived? Miss Marple, that was it. What would she make of this business? From what Gill had told her about him, Cicely couldn't imagine there was anybody like Tommy Boston in St. Mary Mead.

Yet, when you stripped away all the trappings, the television stardom and the Rolls-Royce, wasn't he really quite a common type? A very short man, self-conscious as a boy because of his height, perhaps. And because he was ignorant and not very bright, he had channelled his feeling of inferiority and anger into aggression, making other people look silly to bolster his own ego. Success had only made him worse.

Basically he was a conceited little bully. Rather like Fenning, the butcher in the little town where she had lived before she was married. He couldn't keep his hands to himself either, and in the end it had got him into trouble. He hadn't been murdered, he had gone to prison for dealing on the black market during the war. Rumour had it Charlie Hatton had gone to the police and given him away because Fenning was becoming a bit too familiar with Mrs. Hatton. Charlie was a good-looking, quick-tempered fellow and he was devoted to his wife. A builder.

Cicely pulled herself up short. This was absurd, she thought. Worse, it was dangerous. Yet Trevor could have killed Boston. It wasn't that he was vicious, but there was a violent streak in his make-up, and if he was driven too far . . . The compulsion would have to be very strong, but given it, Cicely believed he would be capable of killing. Only then, of course, the circumstances would probably mean it wouldn't count as murder. She looked from Trevor to Gillian and sighed.

Lambert's lunch had consisted of two thin slices of shiny, slightly damp ham and a limp salad in the canteen.

"From the lab, sir," the constable said, laying a large envelope on his desk.

Lambert thanked him, picked up the envelope and slit it along the top. This would be only a preliminary report, he knew, but it could make or break the theory he was beginning to piece together. If the scientists had found anything which made that theory a nonstarter, he would be back at stage one. Not quite able to stifle his anxiety, he began reading the typed pages.

Part of what he read he didn't understand, there was a good deal of technical language, and no soil had remained on the knife to enable a comparison to be made with that in the wound. The lab hadn't yet received the specimen Lambert had despatched one of his men to take from the flower-bed at Forge Cottage after he received Hewlett's call. There were fibres on Boston's clothing which corresponded with samples from the study carpet, and a very small quantity of a similar material in a crack between two layers of leather in the heel of his right shoe and on his trousers.

There was a good deal more. Lambert read to the end, then turned back and read part of the report again. He breathed a faint sigh of relief. Nothing in it contradicted his ideas. From the file on his desk he extracted the time-table he had drawn up last night and for the next few minutes he studied it.

He had allowed Chester to mislead him. Chester with his talk about detective stories, and who was so vague about times before two-thirty and so sure of them between two-thirty and three. Lambert picked up his phone.

"Ask WPC Graham to come to see me, will you?" he asked the constable who answered it.

"Very good, sir."

Lambert took a fresh sheet of paper from one of the drawers in his desk and started making notes. He had only just begun when there was a tap on the door and Flick walked in.

"You wanted me, sir?" she said.

"Yes." Lambert stood up. "Miss Wareham's remembered something. I told her I'd go to see her at three-thirty; you'd better come too."

"It's very good of you," Mrs. Layton said for the third time in the last twenty minutes.

"Not at all," Hastings assured her again. "I'm only too glad I could help."

He glance at his watch. Ten to three. The old girl hadn't been ready when he called for her. Her husband had said she wouldn't be a minute, but it was nearly five before she appeared, flustered and full of apologies. Not that time mattered, he told himself. All the same, he pressed his foot a little harder on the accelerator.

"I don't often go in a car these days," Mrs. Layton said. "Not since we had to give ours up because it wasn't really safe for George to drive with his eyes. It's quite a treat."

"I'm glad." How easy it was to give pleasure to the very old and the very young, Hastings reflected. He wondered what Carole was doing this afternoon. Aloud he asked, "What will you do about coming back?"

"Oh, I'll manage somehow," Mrs. Layton answered.

Which would probably mean hiring a taxi she couldn't afford. "How long will you be at the home?" Hastings asked her.

"I don't know. It'll be at least an hour, I expect, but it depends how Dora is. If she's bad she may not want me to stay too long."

"I'll bring you home."

"Oh, I couldn't let you do that," the old lady protested. "You've been so good already."

"That's all right," Hastings assured her. "I haven't anything in particular to do this afternoon."

"I don't like to think of you hanging about waiting. You must go and have a cup of tea."

Hastings laughed. "I'll be all right," he said. "You stay as long as you want to. And I hope you'll find your sister's much better today."

"Oh, I hope so." Mrs. Layton groped in her

handbag for a handkerchief. She had hardly spoken to Mr. Hastings before today. What a nice young man he was, she thought. So kind and considerate. It would take such a load off her mind if she knew he was going to take her home.

He's early, Susan told herself when the doorbell rang. Lambert had said three-thirty, and it was still only just after three-fifteen. She was glad. It might be a trivial matter, but she didn't like the feeling that, however unwittingly, she had lied to the police. It would be a relief to tell Lambert about her watch being slow, and once she had explained she could forget all about it.

Putting down the book she had been trying without much success to read for the last hour, she went out to the hall and pressed the button which released the catch on the street door. She heard the door close and footsteps coming up the stairs, and opened the flat door.

She was on the point of saying, "Good afternoon, Superintendent," when she realized her caller wasn't Lambert. She couldn't even tell if it was a man or a woman on the dimly lit landing because he, or she, was wearing a cape which enveloped him from his neck almost to his ankles and a Balaclava helmet concealing everything but his eyes.

She gasped and made a move to shut the door. But before she could do so the grotesque figure raised its right arm. Susan saw something bright in its gloved hand and opened her mouth to scream as the hand plunged down. The strength had ebbed from her limbs and she couldn't move. She felt a violent blow on her chest, and the scream died in her throat. She staggered back. There was a second blow, followed by a searing pain, and she sank to her knees as the figure turned and fled back down the stairs.

Dimly she thought, I'm dying. Oh God, help me somebody! There was a roaring in her ears, then oblivion blotted out everything.

Breckley consisted of a square with a number of streets radiating from it, a score of shops, rather fewer pubs, and three small housing estates. Lambert knew the town from his early days in the force when he had been "on cars" in the division, and he had no difficulty in finding Fore Street. The house was fifty yards along on the right. Parking by the kerb, he looked up at its grey early Victorian front.

Sensible, attractive and well proportioned, he thought. Like Susan Wareham herself.

"Let's see what it is she's remembered," he said to Flick.

There were two bells beside the door. The upper one was labelled in neat capitals "WAREHAM," the lower, in a more rounded handwriting, "MRS. RELPH." Lambert pressed the top one. There was no response, and after a decent interval he rang again. Still nothing happened.

"What do you make the time?" he asked Flick.

"Three thirty-four, sir."

"So do I." Lambert pressed the bell again.

When this third attempt produced no result he tried the lower bell. This time the door was opened almost immediately by a middle-aged woman in glasses wearing a light mack as if she had either just come in or was on the point of going out.

"Yes?" she enquired doubtfully.

"Mrs. Relph?" Lambert asked.

"Yes."

"We're sorry to trouble you, but do you know if Miss Wareham's in? We arranged to call at three-thirty, but we can't get an answer and we wondered if her bell wasn't working."

"It should be," Mrs. Relph said. "I'm afraid I haven't seen her. I've only just come in."

"We're police officers," Lambert told her.

"Oh. There's nothing wrong, is there?" Mrs. Relph looked concerned. "Susan hasn't been burgled or anything?"

Lambert, who hoped very much nothing was wrong, said only, "May we come in, please?"

Mrs. Relph stood aside and he started up the stairs two at a time, Flick not far behind him. Across the tiny landing the door of Susan's flat was open two or three inches. He pushed it cautiously, his anxiety hardening into fear. The door moved only a few inches before stopping against something bulky, but it was enough for Lambert to see a woman lying face down on the floor.

"Stay there," he told Flick curtly.

Squeezing round the door, he squatted beside the prostrate girl. He could see now it was Susan. Her legs were partly drawn up and her arms bent under her, as if she had been clutching her chest when she fell, while an ugly pool of blood was soaking into the carpet.

Lambert felt for her pulse. It was very weak, but she was still breathing.

"Get an ambulance. Quick," he called to Flick, who was waiting anxiously on the landing. "Tell her we've a woman here with severe stab wounds. And ask Inspector Fletcher to send a team."

Flick fled down the stairs and out by the front door. Lambert followed her more slowly as far as the hall and tapped on the door of the ground-floor flat. Mrs. Relph opened it looking worried.

"I'm afraid there's been an accident," he told her.

"Oh no! Not Susan?"

"Yes. Have you any bandages and lint?"

"I don't know," Mrs. Relph answered uncertainly. "I think I have."

She disappeared back into the flat. Lambert waited impatiently, and in a mercifully short time she returned with a large packet of lint and some bandages.

"These are all I've got, I'm afraid," she told him. "Will they do?"

"They'll be fine. Thank you very much," Lambert assured her, taking them and turning back to the stairs.

"Is she all right? What's happened?" Mrs. Relph asked worriedly.

"She's been stabbed. We're sending for an ambulance."

"Oh, how awful!"

Susan was still breathing. Lambert did what he could with the dressings, but it wasn't a great deal because he dared not move her more than absolutely necessary. Thankfully, the external bleeding seemed to have almost stopped. He hoped she wasn't bleeding internally.

He had almost finished when Flick returned. "The ambulance is on its way, sir," she reported. "And Inspector Fletcher is sending a team."

"Good girl." Lambert joined her on the landing. They had done what they could, now the injured woman's fate was out of their hands.

"It's Susan Wareham?" Flick asked.

"Yes. She's pretty bad. It looks as if she was stabbed at least twice—and this time whoever did it didn't leave his knife behind. She's bled a lot." Lambert paused. "Hold the fort here, I want another word with the lady downstairs."

The door of the lower flat was ajar, as if Mrs.

242

Relph expected him to return, and when he tapped on it she appeared at once.

"How is Susan?" she asked.

"Not very well, I'm afraid. I'm Detective Superintendent Lambert. You said you'd just come in, Mrs. Relph. Did you mean a few seconds before or several minutes?"

"About two minutes, I should think. I hadn't even taken my mack off, just opened the windows and given Sandy his milk. Sandy's my cat."

So Lambert had supposed, and as if to demonstrate the fact a large sandy cat insinuated itself round its mistress's legs and stood looking up at him enquiringly.

"Had you been out long?" he asked.

"Since yesterday morning. I went to see a friend at Winchester; she hadn't been very well. Susan said she would look after Sandy. Not that he needs much looking after. Cats don't, do they? They're very independent. I came home earlier than I meant to because I haven't a car and it's so difficult fitting in the trains and buses on a Sunday. There aren't anything like as many as there used to be."

"No," Lambert agreed. "You didn't see anybody about when you came back?"

"I didn't notice anyone," Mrs. Relph answered slowly. More briskly she added, "No, I'm sure there wasn't."

"Miss Wareham hadn't said anything about expecting anybody to come to see her?" Lambert knew that if she had, it was very unlikely the caller she expected had anything to do with the attack on her. He was satisfied that was linked with Boston's murder, and the comedian was still alive when Mrs. Relph left here yesterday.

"No. We don't see very much of each other, you know, really. We're very friendly; she's a sweet girl. She looks after her nephew every Sunday so that his parents can go out together. I think that's very nice in a young girl—but she's a private person, and so am I. It's so much better than living in each other's pockets. The girl who used to have the flat was up and down the whole time, borrowing this or that." Mrs. Relph paused for breath. "I wonder why Susan didn't go round to her sister's this afternoon. Oh, but you said you'd arranged to come, didn't you?"

"Yes," Lambert said. He wondered if her attacker had known about Susan Wareham's usual Sunday-afternoon routine. If so, it looked as if he had known, too, that she wouldn't be adhering to it this afternoon. Had she told anybody? "Do you know where Miss Wareham's sister lives?" he asked.

"Somewhere in Fanhams Road," Mrs. Relph answered. "I'm afraid I don't know the number —but her name's Mrs. Barrett."

Lambert thanked her and went back to the flat upstairs.

"I'll have to stay here," he told Flick. "I want you to take the car and see everybody except Miss Wightman who was at Forge Cottage yesterday. Get an account of their movements since two o'clock this afternoon— and take the names of any people who'll confirm what they say. Tell them Miss Wareham has been attacked and is in a critical condition, but nothing else. All right?"

"Yes, sir."

"I'll see you back at my office when you've finished."

Flick departed eagerly. She was climbing into Lambert's car when the ambulance pulled up.

14

THE house in a quiet road in Barnes had been built in the 1890s. Its grey brick walls were pierced with rectangular, meanly framed windows and there was a semi-circular transom over the front door. Lambert, as he walked up the short drive between rhodo-dendron bushes, reflected that it was strange middle-class Victorians, who set such store by appearances, should have built themselves such outwardly dull and unattractive homes.

The man who answered his ring was stocky and about fifty, with dark wavy hair, a sallow complexion and dark, shrewd eyes. His open-necked shirt and pale blue lightweight trousers gave him the look of a man trying to create an image that was foreign to him and he would have been more at home in a dark suit.

"Superintendent Lambert?" he asked in a pleasant baritone. "Come in, won't you?"

"Thank you for seeing me, Mr. Harford," Lambert said, following him into a largish room lined with bookshelves. The doors, the high ceiling and the iron overmantel were painted white and the only colour was provided by the covers of the books.

"Sit down, Superintendent," Harford said. "Can I get you something to drink?"

"No, thank you all the same." Lambert smiled. "I'm driving."

"Yes, of course. How can I help you?"

"I'm in charge of enquiries into the death of Tommy Boston."

"Oh." Harford brought the tips of his fingers together and regarded Lambert over them. Then, as if it were a habit of which he was slightly ashamed, he dropped his hands to the arms of his chair. "I read about it in the papers this morning. One of my co-directors was staying in the house."

"Yes," Lambert agreed.

"I'm not sure I like this very much—but I appreciate you have your job to do. What do you want to know?"

"I understand your firm published Boston's autobiography."

Harford looked mildly surprised. "Yes, we did. I'm afraid I can't tell you much about it, though. You should ask Alethea."

"She was responsible for it? It was her decision to publish it?"

"In practice, yes. She handles our biographies, and what some misguided people call 'literary fiction,' God help them. I'm the managing director and responsible for our crime list; Dinah Stephenson does art, travel and cookery books; and Justin Vickers deals with sales and the bits and pieces."

"You said 'in practice,'" Lambert commented.

"That's right. It was Alethea's field and her decision, but we all went along with it."

Lambert hesitated. "Would I be speaking out of turn if I said it didn't seem to me the sort of book you usually publish?" he asked.

Harford eyed him curiously. "No, you wouldn't," he said softly. "May I ask why? No, I won't ask, I'd like to think the reason's plain to anyone with taste and common sense."

"There was no particular reason why you took it?" Lambert ignored the implied compliment.

Again the publisher regarded him speculatively. "I take it you aren't asking out of idle curiosity. No. It was the best and worst of all reasons—money. Boston was a big name, he'd

248

just signed a contract for a new television series, and even publishers have to eat. As a matter of fact, we weren't all happy about it; Justin said Boston must have something on Alethea for her to want to take it. I don't suppose I should tell you that, should I? It was only a joke." Harford stopped. "I just can't understand why Logan Chester invited Boston for the weekend after what he did to him."

"What did he do to him?" Lambert asked. This was something new.

"You don't know? I'm not telling tales out of school, it was public enough at the time." Harford explained about Chester's television programme.

Lambert wondered why nobody had mentioned it before. But perhaps that wasn't surprising when you thought about it; the incident had happened some time ago, and people's memories for matters which didn't concern them personally were very short. Those members of the party at Forge Cottage who knew—and besides Chester himself, Susan Wareham and Alethea Wightman at least must surely have done—had decided to say nothing.

"Miss Wightman's been with your firm a long time, hasn't she?" he said.

"Donkey's years. She started as a secretary, her family were nothing to do with the trade. I don't know what we'd do without her now." Harford smiled. "I think she still looks on me as a new boy, to be tolerated and manoeuvred, but never deferred to."

Lambert, visualizing Alethea at a board meeting, laughed.

He had acquired two more items of information, he reflected as he got back into his car a little later. First, Alethea Wightman had pressed for her firm to bring out Boston's autobiography against the opposition of at least some of the other directors. Pressed so hard, indeed, that one of them had laughingly suggested Boston must have a hold over her. Second, Boston had publicly and deliberately made a fool of Chester. True, it had happened some time ago, but Lambert couldn't see Chester accepting such treatment meekly, or with a good grace.

"It looks as if the Wareham girl was telling the truth," Beeley reported. "Rayment, the man who runs the post office, confirms what she says about going there yesterday afternoon and staying several minutes talking to his wife. And the old lady, Miss Rider, says she was with her at least ten minutes. Not that it makes much difference now."

"Probably not," Lambert agreed. "She certainly didn't inflict those injuries herself."

He wondered what it was Susan Wareham had remembered that she had been going to tell him that afternoon. He should have let her tell him on the phone, only he had wanted to watch her while she told him, to see whether she betrayed by any tiny sign that she was lying.

With luck he should know soon; the latest news from the hospital was that she had undergone an emergency operation, and not yet come round from the anaesthetic. Although she had lost a lot of blood, the knife had missed any vital organ, and she should be out of bed in a few days. A woman constable was with her now, waiting for her to recover consciousness.

"That post office is a real old village store," Beeley went on.

"I know," Lambert said, "they sell kitchen knives."

The sergeant looked disappointed. He had been looking forward to bringing out that piece of information and surprising the boss.

Lambert saw his expression and grinned. "Chester told us," he explained.

"He would," Beeley said disgustedly. "They're on a card just inside the door, and the biggest two are missing. But Rayment says he sold them weeks ago, and nobody has asked for one since then. His wife confirms it. They're certain none's been nicked, either. The ones on the card are the only ones they've had for months."

"Chester seems to think one of his guests made up his mind to kill Boston during lunch, slipped across to the post office when nobody was looking, got hold of one of the knives— legitimately or otherwise—and went back and stabbed him. At least, that's the theory he's putting forward; he's too intelligent to believe it."

"Good of him," Beeley commented.

"He's very helpful," Flick said.

"Whoever killed Boston planned it before they got to the cottage yesterday. Unless it was Chester. They brought the knife with them, and stuck it in the flower-bed by the side door ready for use when the opportunity came," Lambert said. He paused. "Inspector Fletcher still hasn't had any joy tracing the call Boston's supposed to have made, and so far the house-to-house hasn't turned up anything. I don't suppose we can hope for anything more at Breckley. One interesting thing has come out today, though."

"What's that, sir?" Beeley asked.

"We know now that Susan Wareham hated Boston, and why. Three years ago he nearly killed her nephew. His car mounted the pavement and knocked him down when he was out with his mother. The little boy was not quite six, and he suffered severe brain damage; he'll be little better than a vegetable for the rest of his life. The doctors say he won't live beyond twenty-five, and he's the only child. Boston was breathalyzed and found positive, but he'd pulled the old stunt and had a stiff scotch from a flask he kept in the car, to 'steady his nerves' after the accident. He claimed he'd had to swerve to avoid another car coming in the opposite direction. The kid's mother admitted there was another car, but she was sure it hadn't done anything to make him swerve. It was his word against hers, there wasn't enough evidence to convict him and he got off.

"Miss Wareham is very fond of the boy, her sister says. She goes to be with him nearly every Sunday afternoon so that his parents can have some time to themselves. Every time she sees him, she must be reminded of what Boston did."

"No wonder she hated him," Flick said.

"And she's the only one who knew the Bostons were going to be there yesterday before she left home." Lambert stopped. "There was a mixed bag of knives in her kitchen."

"But she can't have killed Boston," Beeley objected.

"Perhaps not," Lambert agreed.

The others waited, but he said no more, and after a moment Beeley went on, "There were several knives in the Bostons' kitchen. Two of them were the right make and smaller; Mrs. Boston says she's never had any bigger ones, for what that's worth. Hastings had four knives, different sorts and sizes."

"I managed to get hold of Boston's solicitor this evening," Lambert said. "Boston left everything to his wife. The solicitor wasn't very forthcoming, but I gathered it wasn't as much as you might think; Boston spent a lot, and the tax man had caught up with him. Still, it'll be a tidy sum. There's something else: Boston rang him a fortnight ago and said he wanted to make a new will, but he didn't say what he wanted to change, and he hadn't done anything about it."

"Mrs. Boston has a boy-friend," Beeley told him. "Their house is part of a big old rectory, and I talked to a couple of the people in the other parts. One of them said, the last few months they were always having rows. The boy-friend came two or three times when Boston was away. He drives an old brown Maxi."

"Peter Hastings," Flick said.

Lambert nodded. "What did you find out about them, Roger?"

"Not a lot," Beeley admitted. "Carole Boston's father was a greengrocer in South London and she went straight from school into a dance group. She got her job in that television quiz show about a year ago and there's nothing known against her. Hastings worked in an insurance office before he became a journalist. Then he was a reporter on a local rag in Kent for a while. He moved on without ever making a name for himself, and finished up on one of the big provincial papers. People seem to like him, but they say he's too quiet and shy to make many friends. So far I haven't found out anything we didn't already know about Chester, but Jack Tomlin's dug up something on Lane.

He hasn't any details yet, but it seems he and Boston were both involved in some property deal a year or so ago. It went wrong, and Boston wriggled out, leaving Lane to carry the can. He's supposed to have lost nearly thirty thousand pounds."

"Is he?" Lambert said. "That's interesting."

"Mrs. Lane's father was a doctor, consultant at a big hospital and a practice in Harley Street. She started training as a nurse, but she was ill and jacked it in. After that she worked in PR for a hotel group."

Lambert turned to Flick. "What were they all doing this afternoon?"

"Mrs. Lane says she was at home," the girl replied. "Mr. Lane had been going to play cricket, but he scrubbed that and drove Mrs. Boston home; she stayed with them last night. They both say they left about half past two and got there just before three. According to the Lanes, he got back about three-thirty."

"He'd gone when I got to the Bostons' just after three," Beeley said.

Lambert was thinking. "Half an hour each way. It's about eighteen miles; I suppose that's reasonable. He must have spent a minute or two there, he'd hardly push her out and drive straight home. Still, it's not exactly hurrying, he'd have had time to stab Miss Wareham. Breckley would have been on his way."

"There's nothing to confirm Mrs. Lane's story, Mrs. Robins was out and didn't get back until nearly four," Flick said, turning a page of her notebook. "Hastings took an old lady named Layton to Wittenham to see her sister in an old people's home. They both say they got there just before three. She was with her sister for about an hour, and when she came out he was waiting for her. He could have driven to Breckley, attacked Susan Wareham, and driven back again, but he'd only arranged to take the old girl when he heard her husband complaining about there being no buses when he was in the pub at lunch-time."

"That's not conclusive," Lambert said.

"No, sir."

"Alethea Wightman doesn't drive. That doesn't rule her out, but it makes it less likely she was at Breckley. Which leaves us with Logan Chester."

"He seemed really shocked. He could have been putting it on, I suppose—and he asked me twice if she'd been able to tell us who attacked her. He said he was at home all the afternoon, working on a new book," Flick said.

"So any of them could have done it," Lambert mused. "Except Mrs. Boston. What we need to know is *why* they tried to kill her —and why it was necessary to rig the locked room. Perhaps Miss Wareham will be able to tell us."

"Both things, sir?" Beeley asked. He sounded surprised.

"If we're lucky."

"What about how the room was worked?"

"I think I know that," Lambert replied. Beeley and Flick stared at him. "I'd like to know who Chester's protecting."

"Himself?" Flick suggested.

"Maybe. I can't see him sticking his neck out for Miss Wightman or Lane. The obvious person is Miss Wareham, but now it looks as if she didn't kill Boston—and if you eliminate her, you're left with Mrs. Lane and Mrs. Boston, neither of whom can have done it. So we're back to Chester himself. The interesting thing, if he did it, is why he was so emphatic Boston must have been stabbed between two thirty-two and three-oh-two when he hadn't an alibi for the first eight minutes. And why is he so vague about times before two-thirty, and so sure about them after then?"

"Because something happened then, and he saw times were important," Flick suggested.

"That's obvious," Beeley told her.

"But what was it?" Lambert wanted to know. "At two thirty-two Boston was still alive."

"Chester knew he was going to kill him," Beeley ventured. "It could be. But if that's it, he's going to extraordinary lengths to put us off the track, asking questions at the pub about the time Lane left, and all the rest of it. He says the study's being locked is the most important aspect of the whole business, but for all his playing at detectives, he doesn't tell us how or why it was done. Either he doesn't know or he daren't tell us because it would give too much away."

"He's too clever by half," Beeley grumbled.

"Oh, he is. All the same, I have an idea at least part of it's an act he's putting on for our benefit."

Lambert stopped. Suddenly, without thinking about it, he had remembered the idea he had had before Dr. Hewlett telephoned that morning. He must talk to Susan Wareham.

"You two had better go home," he said. "There's nothing more we can do tonight."

They said goodnight and went out together. Lambert stayed a few minutes longer, then he, too, packed up and went home, to the semi-detached house on the other side of Wittenham he and Barbara had bought seven years before. When she left him he had considered selling it and moving into a flat, but something—perhaps a faint hope he wouldn't own, even to himself, that one day she would come back—had stopped him. By increasing the mortgage and realizing most of his savings, he had succeeded in scraping together enough to pay her for her share.

Too weary to bother with getting himself a proper meal, still less to go out for one, he cut a thick slice from a loaf, spread it with butter and took a block of supermarket Stilton from the refrigerator. But the bread was stale and the cheese still hard and tasteless from the fridge. He ate only a little of it, then pushed his plate aside, fetched a can of beer and settled down to think.

The case was beginning to form a pattern. Little pieces of information were fitting together. He had been on the right track, then

Dr. Hewlett called, and by the time he put down the phone the idea had gone. What was it Hewlett had said? Something about Boston having eaten a nice piece of Stilton. As if he could tell. Lambert eyed the half-eaten piece of cheese on his plate.

"Oh no!" he breathed. The truth had been staring them in the face all the time, and none of them had seen it.

Now the pattern was almost complete. Yet it was so extraordinary, so bizarre, that even now he found it hard to accept it. He went over and over it in his mind, trying to find loopholes in it, but there were none. He knew now how the murder had been committed, and why the locked room was necessary; all that remained was the identity of the murderer.

Lambert went out to the hall and fetched the typescript of Gillian Lane's novel from his case. It was after midnight before he went to bed, and by then he had read enough to satisfy himself that a man like Trevor Lane might well have reacted violently when he knew what the book was about. But why vent his rage on Boston? The failed property deal, taken with the comedian's behaviour to Lane's wife yesterday, provided a far more likely motive.

15

IT seemed to Lambert he had only just fallen asleep when the telephone by his bed rang, waking him. He rolled over and lifted the receiver.

"Superintendent Lambert, sir?" It was Sergeant Tilling from divisional HQ. Susan Wareham had recovered consciousness and the doctor said they could talk to her for a few minutes.

"I'll be there in a quarter of an hour," Lambert said.

Fourteen minutes later he parked in a space marked "DOCTORS ONLY" outside the main block of Wittenham General Hospital. He couldn't see many doctors needing the available spaces during the next twenty minutes.

"Through that door, up the stairs, along the corridor on your left, and Marchmont Ward's the last door on your right," the porter told him.

Lambert took the stairs two at a time. Beyond them the long corridor was deserted and in semidarkness. Through the glass panes in the doors he passed he could see the dim glow of heavily shaded lights. It was a strange sensation, he thought, walking through this vast building, knowing that within a few yards of him two or three hundred people were lying, yet hearing no sound. It reminded him of nights years ago when, a young constable in Traffic, all too often it had fallen to him to come to hospitals like this after motor accidents. More recently, tiptoeing with Barbara along a corridor almost identical with this one that dreadful night when they had been called because what had seemed to be a fairly serious but not dangerous illness in a boy of five had suddenly become a crisis, then a loss, stunning in its completeness and its unexpectedness.

Barbara had changed after that. She couldn't, or wouldn't, understand how he could carry on with his work and seem to put their tragedy behind him, almost, at times, as if he had forgotten it. That he had to give so much of himself to his job, not only because it was demanded of him, but because that was his way of coming to terms with life. The only way he knew. And because she hadn't understood, she resented it more than anything else. Perhaps, too, she had envied his having that rock to hold on to when she, without great faith or absorbing interests, couldn't find one. Had he failed her then?

Lambert pushed the memories away and silently opened the door of Marchmont Ward. As he did so a staff nurse seated at a table near the door looked up.

"I'm Detective Superintendent Lambert," he told her softly.

The girl smiled. "Oh, yes. Miss Wareham's in the side ward on the left at the end. You can go along, but you won't keep her talking long, will you? And don't upset her."

"No," Lambert promised. "She's all right, though, isn't she?"

"Would you be all right if you'd had a knife stuck right into you twice?" It was surprising how caustic the nurse could make a mere whisper sound. "She should be in a few days."

Lambert nodded his thanks and tiptoed along the ward between the two rows of beds. One of the patients was snoring gently. There was a shaded light on in the side ward and Susan Wareham, very pale and still, was lying with her eyes open. When Lambert came in she turned her head lethargically, and the woman constable stood up.

"I'll take your chair if I may," he told her. It was the only one there, and he didn't want to talk to the injured girl while he was standing looming over her. The WPC moved a few steps to one side and he sat down. "Do you remember me, Miss Wareham?"

Susan nodded weakly. "You're Superintendent Lambert. I rang you."

"Yes. How do you feel?"

"Sore rather. And horribly weak. But not too bad, I suppose, considering."

"You know what happened?"

"Part of it."

"Did you see who attacked you?"

"Not properly. He was wearing a sort of cape and a Balaclava."

Ye gods! Lambert thought. "You're sure it was a man though?" he asked.

Susan hesitated. "No. I just took it for granted it was. But it could have been a woman. It was all so quick, and I could only see their eyes."

So much for Felicity Graham's hopes, Lambert reflected. His, too, come to that. If Susan Wareham couldn't tell if her attacker was a man or a woman, clearly she had no idea as to his or her identity.

"You said on the phone you wanted to tell me something," he reminded her gently.

"It wasn't anything much. Just that I remembered my watch was five minutes slow yesterday and it was really a quarter to three when I got back from the post office and Miss Rider's, not twenty to. Does it make any difference?"

Clearly she had been worrying about her mistake, and Lambert thought he knew why.

"I shouldn't think so," he replied, not altogether truthfully. Changing the subject, he asked, "Do you remember, you told me you had to go round to the kitchen because the side door was sticking?"

"Yes."

"Where did it stick?"

"At the top. That's where it always does."

"So Miss Hemmings told us. And I found it did when I tried it yesterday morning. But it was only sticking slightly, I could open it quite easily, and Mr. Lane came in that way when he came back from the Wheatsheaf. Are you sure that's where it stuck when you tried it on Saturday afternoon?"

Lambert saw the bewilderment in the girl's eyes. She's remembered, he thought.

"No, it wasn't," Susan told him. "It was in the middle."

"By the lock, you mean?"

"Yes. It wasn't sticking, was it? It was locked. I was so used to it sticking I didn't think. But who can have locked it? And why?"

Lambert suspected she had already guessed the answer to the first question. "I don't know yet—and it may not mean anything," he replied, despising himself a little for his second half-truth. She would worry, and perhaps that would be his fault, but he had had to know.

Outside in the ward a woman cried out in her sleep, the sound startling and somehow eerie after the silence. Lambert saw Susan start. No wonder if her nerves were on edge, he thought.

"Can you remember, when you and Mr. Chester were getting the drinks to take out to the garden, did either of you leave the kitchen, even for just a few seconds?" he asked.

"Logan did." Susan frowned. "He went to get some more glasses from the dining-room. But he was only gone a minute."

Lambert nodded. "Did you tell anybody who

else was going to be there on Saturday, Miss Wareham?"

"Tell anybody?" Susan repeated. "No. Why should I? Anyway, Logan didn't tell me until Friday afternoon."

"That's all then, thank you." Lambert smiled reassuringly and stood up. "I'm sorry I had to bother you tonight, but it was rather important."

The staff nurse came in looking businesslike.

"I was just leaving," Lambert told her, making a move towards the door.

"Mr. Lambert," Susan said, "I saw Alethea Wightman."

Lambert turned back. "When?"

"Yesterday afternoon. She was in the street outside the flat. It was soon after you rang me back; Logan called to suggest we went out somewhere for dinner. Oh." Susan stopped. "He must have come for me and wondered where I was."

Lambert saw no need to tell her that Chester wouldn't have gone, because by then he had heard from Felicity Graham what had happened. Apparently he had been terribly shocked.

268

"When I put the phone down I glanced out of the window, and she was there," Susan said.

The nurse was uncertain whether to intervene and send Lambert away, but decided it would be better to let her patient get whatever it was off her mind.

"It can't have been her, can it?" the girl said.

"I don't know," Lambert told her, "but we'll find out. When Mr. Chester rang, did you tell him about your watch being slow?"

"Yes."

"And that I was coming to see you at three-thirty?"

"Yes." Susan looked horrified. "But it can't . . . You're wrong."

"You must go, Superintendent," the nurse said angrily.

"Don't worry, Miss Wareham," Lambert said. He walked back through the sleeping ward and out to the corridor. More pieces were falling into place.

Alethea Wightman's office was on the fifth floor of a block not far from the British Museum. The block had been built in the thirties and now had a slightly seedy appearance, as if nobody cared much about it, and soon it would start sliding unnoticed into the first stages of decay.

Lambert consulted the board in the lobby and pressed the button for the lift, which wheezed and rattled upwards to the fourth floor. The girl at the reception desk was knitting herself a pink jumper from a pattern in a magazine. She gave Lambert a friendly smile, put down her knitting and asked if she could help him.

"I'd like to see Miss Wightman," he told her.

"Have you an appointment?"

"No."

"I'm sorry she doesn't see anybody without an appointment," the girl said. "I'll tell her secretary; maybe she can help. What name shall I say?"

"Detective Superintendent Lambert," Lambert told her. "And it's Miss Wightman I want to see."

The receptionist hesitated, apparently decided the wrath of the police was less to be feared than Alethea's and picked up her telephone.

"Deirdre? There's a Detective Superintendent here to see Miss Wightman," she said.

The phone crackled indignantly.

"I know. I told him." She put it down. "Her secretary's coming. She won't be a minute."

Lambert resigned himself to the inevitable and passed the four minutes before the secretary arrived studying the shelves of the firm's latest publications. Boston's autobiography wasn't amongst them. Perhaps Harford and the other directors had counter-attacked.

The secretary, a plump, homely-looking woman, gave him a curious look and said, "Miss Wightman can see you now. Will you come this way?"

Lambert followed her up a steep staircase to Alethea's office. It was quite small and sparsely furnished with a desk, behind which Alethea sat in a large executive chair, and two more, much less comfortable chairs she had selected herself with the object of deterring any visitors from staying too long.

The secretary said, "Detective Superintendent Lambert, Miss Wightman," and departed.

Alethea regarded him with cool hostility. "I can't think there is anything more I could tell you which would conceivably help your enquiries, Superintendent," she said.

"There are just one or two more questions I

have to ask you in the light of certain developments since Saturday," Lambert told her, not in the least put out by her manner.

Alethea's discriminating eyebrows rose. "Oh?" she said. "I can't imagine what they can be about."

"First, would you tell me where you were yesterday afternoon between two-thirty and three-thirty?"

"Yesterday afternoon? What on earth can that have to do with that dreadful business on Saturday?"

"Would you just tell me where you were?" Lambert asked politely.

Alethea eyed him resentfully but decided it would be as well to answer, however unnecessary and impertinent the question might seem. "I was at home," she said.

"All the time?"

"Yes. I didn't feel inclined for company."

"And you saw nobody during that time?"

"No. Why are you asking about yesterday? Has something else happened?"

"Miss Wareham was attacked in her flat about three o'clock yesterday," Lambert replied.

"And you think I may have had something to do with it?" Alethea was outraged.

"We have to check every possibility," Lambert told her calmly. "However remote it may seem."

"I assure you I know nothing about it," Alethea said icily. "Was she hurt?"

"She was stabbed twice. She's in hospital in a serious condition, but she's expected to be about again in a few days."

"I'm glad, she always seemed a nice girl." Alethea's tone hardly suggested much concern. "Far too good for Logan Chester."

"If we might get back to Saturday," Lambert said. "There's nothing you would like to add to what you said in your statement, that you were in your room all the time from lunch until Mr. Chester came to tell you Mr. Boston had been killed?"

"No. Why should there be?"

Lambert ignored the question. "Miss Wightman, why did you hate Tommy Boston?"

"He was rude, boastful and vulgar. Impossible in every way."

"That would explain dislike; you hated him."

Alethea hesitated. "I will admit I disliked him intensely. He came here once when we were publishing his wretched autobiography. He hadn't an appointment, he was very drunk and he assaulted my secretary. It wasn't a very serious assault, but the whole incident was extremely unpleasant. I wanted to call the police, but she was afraid she would have to give evidence in court, and in the end I let her persuade me."

"Was that the girl I saw just now?" Lambert asked.

"No, this was Victoria; she left a few months ago. She was a pleasant girl, rather old-fashioned, and the experience affected her badly."

"I'm not surprised." Lambert paused. "Why did you publish Boston's book?"

"Why shouldn't we?" Alethea demanded, hackles rising.

Lambert felt like saying "Oh, come!" but resisted the temptation, and answered instead, "It's not the sort of book you usually publish. It's rather unpleasant, and badly written."

Alethea glared at him, and he knew he had touched a tender spot; he had questioned her literary judgement. Probably she was particularly sensitive about that book.

"I didn't realize you were qualified to be a

critic," she said icily. "We published it because we believed it would sell. It has."

"That was the only reason?"

There was no double glazing at the window and Lambert could hear the rumble of traffic in the street while he waited for Alethea to answer. When she did her tone had changed.

"I suppose I have to tell you. We're a perfectly sound company financially, but at that time all publishers were finding things difficult. We had had several expensive books which hadn't done as well as we expected, and we took the decision to broaden our market by publishing more 'popular' books. Boston's was one of them."

Lambert remembered Martin Harford saying, "Even publishers have to eat," and decided Alethea was probably telling the truth. It must have gone against the grain for her to make that admission about her beloved company.

"Thank you," he said, standing up. "I hope I shan't have to trouble you again."

"So do I," Alethea agreed tartly. "Good day, Superintendent." She watched Lambert go out of the room, waited until the door closed behind him, then picked up her telephone. "Get me

Logan Chester," she told the girl on the switchboard.

"We still don't know why Susan Wareham was attacked," Lambert said.

"Something the murderer discovered she knew?" Beeley suggested.

"That's the most likely reason. But if so, it's either something she isn't aware of herself or something she won't admit to knowing. With any luck we'll be able to talk to her again tomorrow, and she may have remembered more by then. Look, the only people who knew in advance Boston would be there on Saturday were his wife, Chester and Miss Wareham. Chester swears he didn't tell anybody but her, and she says she didn't mention it to anyone. They agree she didn't know until Friday lunchtime herself." Lambert stopped. "You know, there's one person we haven't considered in all this."

"Elsie Hemmings!" Flick exclaimed.

"Yes. I'm not suggesting she had anything to do with the murder, but we should have solid grounds for ruling her out. It's just possible she heard Chester telling Miss Wareham who was coming, and she could have brought a knife with her that morning—or taken one from the kitchen, for that matter. Chester wouldn't miss it."

"She may not have gone home as early as she said," Flick remarked. "Hastings said he thought she was in the kitchen when he went to the pub."

"So he did," Lambert agreed thoughtfully.

"What motive could she have had?" Beeley wanted to know. "I still think it was Chester killed Boston."

"Have you any firm evidence, or are you letting yourself be influenced by your dislike of him?" Lambert asked.

"No. He's the one who's been making everything so complicated all the way along. Why's he done that if he hasn't something to hide? It always comes back to him: it was his party, he invited the Bostons, he knew Miss Wightman and Miss Wareham and Hastings hated Boston. Lane, too. He set the whole thing up. He's the expert on detective stories."

"What was his motive?" Lambert asked.

"Boston sloshed up his programme on telly and made him look a berk. I can't see Chester taking that lying down. The way Boston behaved at lunch put the cap on it."

It wasn't terribly convincing, Lambert thought, but the motive for murder often seemed pathetically inadequate to other people. "All right," he said, "how did he fix the locked room?"

Beeley grinned. "I don't know how, but I'm bloody sure he did. He knew Boston was going to be there, and we know now he had nearly a quarter of an hour alone in the kitchen before Miss Wareham came back. Everything was ready, he can't have been getting the drinks all that time."

Lambert reflected that there was a good deal in what Beeley was saying. Only he didn't go far enough.

"I don't think it was Chester," Flick said brightly.

"Why not?" the sergeant demanded. "Feminine intuition?"

"No." Flick ignored the sarcasm. "I know he's vain and thinks he's cleverer than anyone else—especially us—but would he really kill Boston just because of what he did on that show? After all, it was months ago. Besides—"

"You don't know what—" Beeley began scathingly.

Lambert interrupted him. "Let her have her say," he said.

"Well," Flick continued bravely, ignoring Beeley's expression, "if he did it himself, he wouldn't be protecting somebody else, would he? At least," she persisted, floundering slightly and avoiding Lambert's eye—if he looked disapproving it would be bad enough, but amused or sympathetic would be worse—"it's less likely he would. I mean, he'd be only too pleased for somebody else to be suspected, wouldn't he?"

"Somebody," Lambert agreed, "but perhaps not anybody."

"Sir?"

"Well, he might be glad for some people to be under suspicion, but not one particular person. Miss Wareham, for instance."

"Oh," Flick said, looking a little deflated.

"If it's her he's shielding, he wouldn't do that unless he believed she killed Boston, or was involved in his death somehow. Perhaps I'm wrong, and he isn't protecting anybody but himself. We can't get away from the fact that he was the only one who knew she was going to tell us something, and when I was going to see her."

"And what she'd remembered destroyed part of his alibi," Beeley added.

"That's right," Lambert agreed.

"We can count her out now, can't we?"

"Probably. But we can't be absolutely sure until we know somebody else is the murderer. It's even possible the attack on her had nothing to do with Boston's death. It may have been some junkie looking for money for drugs. I'm not saying it's likely, but we can't rule it out as a possibility."

The magnificent basket of flowers on the table beside Susan's bed made the roses she had brought look pathetic, Flick thought. But the girl in the bed thanked her warmly. Already there was more colour in her cheeks and she looked brighter.

"They're gorgeous," Flick commented enthusiastically, bending over to smell the splendid array. There was no card she could see. "Were they from your boy-friend?"

Susan smiled. "I haven't one. Mr. Chester sent them."

"He must think a lot of you."

"He's very kind. He likes giving presents to people."

So had Boston once, to Carole, Flick thought. "You're lucky to have him for a boss," she said, sitting down beside the bed. The uniformed WPC had taken advantage of her coming to go for a cup of tea.

"I am."

"He'd do a good deal to help one of his friends if they were in trouble, wouldn't he?"

Susan looked puzzled. "Yes, I suppose he would," she agreed.

"And he likes you a lot. He must do," Flick said.

A flush came to Susan's cheeks. "I don't know," she murmured. "I shouldn't think so."

"It's obvious he does. That's why he's protecting you."

"Protecting me?" Susan frowned. "What do you mean?"

"You don't know?"

"No. I've no idea what you're talking about. If he'd been protecting me, I might not be here now."

"I didn't mean that sort of protection," Flick told her. "He thinks you killed Tommy Boston, doesn't he?"

"He *can't*!" Susan breathed.

"Why not?"

"He knows I wouldn't do a thing like that. Why should I?"

"Because of what Boston did to your nephew," Flick said. "You're very fond of him, aren't you?"

Susan gazed at her, horror in her eyes. Then, suddenly, she burst into tears.

16

FLICK waited. After a few seconds the sobbing subsided and Susan wiped her eyes.

"I hardly ever do that," she muttered.

"You've been through a lot," Flick told her. "And you've been under a lot of strain these last few days."

Susan supposed that was true. "I am fond of Simon," she said. "He was such a lovely little boy, so full of life. Now . . ."

"How long has Mr. Chester known about him?" Flick asked.

"I told him on Friday, when he said he'd invited the Bostons for the weekend. I told him he couldn't; then I had to explain." Susan hesitated. "What did you mean about him protecting me?"

"It doesn't matter now. Don't worry about it," Flick told her. "It looks certain that the person who attacked you was the same person who killed Tommy Boston; are you sure you didn't notice anything about them? Just whether it was a man or a woman? Anything?"

Susan shook her head. "I didn't. I've been trying to remember, but there's nothing. I took it for granted it was a man."

"Because you thought you knew who it might be?"

"No."

"The thing he or she was wearing, was it a woman's cape?"

"I don't know. I only saw him for a few seconds, and I didn't think." All she had seen was that obscene woollen mask, the eyes glinting through its slits, and the knife clasped in an upraised hand. Had they been a woman's eyes? She couldn't remember seeing any make-up, and the Balaclava hid the eyebrows. Susan shuddered.

"Men don't often wear capes these days," Flick remarked. "Not even policemen and cyclists."

"It was the thing over his face, the Balaclava. You take it for granted anybody wearing one's a man."

That was true, Flick told herself. Balaclavas were associated with troops on active service and armed robbers. And there was something

284

else: anybody confronted with a bizarrely dressed figure, a knife gripped in its upraised fist, was likely to believe their attacker was bigger than he really was. At the same time, both Logan Chester and Trevor Lane were big men, and Alethea Wightman was tall for a woman, while a cape would disguise her thinness. Was it Alethea Susan had seen outside her flat earlier?

"I'm sorry," she said, "but can you try to remember? You saw this hand, was it wearing a glove?"

A glove? Yes, Susan thought. Black fingers wrapped round the handle of the knife. Ugh!

"Yes, a black one," she said. "Leather, I think."

"Good. Whoever it was believed you were a threat to them; did you say anything to anybody about the murder? Anything that might have led them to think you knew who killed Tommy Boston?"

"I had no idea who killed him." Susan hesitated. Something she had remembered had been bothering her while she was lying here with nothing to do, but it was so trivial. "There was one thing," she said. "It's nothing much, just something somebody said to me."

"Do you think they really know anything?" Gillian asked, a note of desperation in her voice.

"How should I know?" Trevor retorted.

"That girl, coming here asking where we were yesterday afternoon. As if the police thought one of us—"

"They'll have gone to everybody." Gill sounded as if her nerve was cracking, Trevor thought, and he had enough to cope with without that.

"But if the others can prove where they were—"

"For God's sake!"

"All right, I'm afraid," Gillian said, her voice pitched higher than usual. "Why shouldn't I be?"

Trevor hesitated before he said, "The superintendent was looking at those books I got from the library. He pretended he was just picking them up casually, but I reckon he'd looked at them while you were coming to fetch me. I said they were mine, and he asked if I'd read them."

"What did you tell him?"

"That I had. He didn't ask about you."

286

"Oh God!" Gillian breathed.

"They can't make anything out of that," Trevor protested.

Gillian gazed at him.

At that moment the telephone rang. Trevor crossed the room and picked it up.

"Hallo?" he said.

Gillian couldn't hear what the caller said, nor recognize the voice. The conversation was brief. When it was over, Trevor replaced the phone and turned back to her. Under his tan his face was pale.

"That was Chester," he said. "He wants us to go round there this evening."

"We can't," Gillian muttered.

"He said he thought we should. It sounded like . . ."

"What?"

"A threat."

"What did you tell him?"

"That we would," Trevor said.

"What the hell did you think you were doing?" Beeley demanded. "Going to see one of the boss's chief witnesses without permission and questioning her about the case. Who do you think you are, Graham?"

287

"I'm sorry, I just didn't think," Flick said humbly. She knew Beeley's anger was justified, and this time she really was chastened. She had come in this evening so full of what she had learnt from Susan Wareham, and now she'd been brought down to earth with a cruel bump. "I thought it would be a nice gesture to take her some flowers, and while I was there, well, the super said we had to know why she was stabbed, and I thought she might talk more freely to another girl. I got carried away, I suppose," she said.

"Didn't it occur to you she's a suspect? You could have ruined everything talking to her." Beeley gazed at Flick in disbelief. "I hate to think what Mr. Lambert will say when he knows. Ten to one you'll be out of here and back on the beat tomorrow."

"Yes, Sergeant," Flick muttered. She wouldn't cry, she told herself furiously. It was her own fault, and she wouldn't give Beeley that satisfaction.

"You'd better report to Inspector Fletcher, and keep your head down, right?"

"Right, Sergeant," Flick said, and hurried away.

"What was all that about?" Lambert

enquired, coming round the corner as Flick disappeared into the murder room. "Our WPC Graham looks as if she's got her tail well and truly between her legs."

"She's just a bit upset; her first murder and all that. Women!" Beeley added significantly.

Lambert eyed him curiously but said nothing. If the sergeant didn't want to tell him, he wasn't going to press him to.

"Have you heard what Miss Wareham's remembered, sir?" Beeley asked.

"No. What's that?" Lambert forgot about Flick.

Beeley told him.

"Where did you learn that?"

"It came from the hospital, sir. I took it you'd heard. I'm sorry, there must have been a cock-up somewhere."

"There must," Lambert agreed. Something to do with WPC Graham, he supposed. He was glad Roger Beeley had dealt with whatever it was without making a major issue of it. "We might as well call it a day," he said. "There's nothing more we can do tonight." The phone on his desk rang and he picked it up. "Lambert."

"Mr. Logan Chester wants to speak to you, sir," the telephonist told him.

"Blast!" Lambert said. "All right, put him through."

Watching, Beeley saw his expression harden as he listened.

"I was just going home," Lambert said shortly. "Has something happened?" The line crackled. "Have you anything new to tell us?" The line crackled again. "Very well." Lambert sighed audibly. "Goodbye."

"That was Chester," he told Beeley. "He wants us to go over there right away. You'd better get Graham to take notes. I'll see you both outside in five minutes."

Thunder rumbled in the distance as they drove past the cottages on the north side of the green and turned down the hill. No lights showed in the Lanes' house, and Oriel Cottage, too, was in darkness. Lambert's misgivings increased.

"What do you think he's up to?" Beeley asked.

"I wish I knew. I don't like it," the superintendent told him.

Chester wouldn't dare try, would he? He had explained nothing on the phone, merely said something was happening, and he thought Lambert should come over at once.

"If he's trying to turn it all into a detective story . . . ," Flick ventured.

"It isn't a story," Lambert told her curtly. "That's the mistake he's made all along."

He pulled up outside Forge Cottage as thunder rolled again, closer this time. Through the trees in Chester's orchard the three in the car could see the setting sun almost obscured by angry white-edged clouds. The breeze which had been blowing earlier had dropped and it was very close.

A bright red Ford Escort Ghia was parked on the drive behind Boston's Rolls.

"That's Carole Boston's car," Beeley said.

The darkness which had covered the other houses like a shroud didn't extend to Forge Cottage; there was a light showing through the curtains at the study windows, and another shining across the lawn from the drawing-room.

"Right," Lambert said. "Come on."

They got out.

"'Strewth, it's hot!" Beeley muttered. He looked up at the front of the house.

"You know what to do," Lambert said. The case was nearly over, he thought. That brought a slight relaxation, yet at the same time he was aware of a new tension. Nothing must go wrong now. "I don't suppose we'll have any trouble, and we know who to watch. Let's just hope Chester isn't planning anything theatrical."

The other two followed him up the short path to the front door. Behind them a car drove up the road, its headlights carving a tunnel of light through the deepening dusk.

Lambert rang the bell. Flick was conscious of the tension inside her and supposed she was nervous, although she didn't feel afraid.

Then Chester opened the door. He was dressed a little more formally this evening in a shirt with a dark red tie and light tan trousers.

"Oh, there you are!" he greeted them warmly. "Three of you, I say. Come in."

He's on a high, Flick thought. Does he take the stuff?

Lambert, with his longer experience, suspected the other man was merely keyed up by the prospect of his own success.

Chester stepped aside for them to walk past him into the hall, but Lambert didn't move.

"I don't know what you have in mind," he said, "but if it's what I suspect it is, I warn you, it's very unwise. It may even constitute an offence."

"I hardly think so. And if we only did what was wise . . ."

"You mean to go ahead?"

"I don't know what it is you think I intend doing." Chester smiled broadly. "But the answer's yes."

"Very well," Lambert told him. "In that case I want the side door locked, and I want the key."

Chester eyed him thoughtfully, then he shrugged. "If you think that's necessary."

"I do."

Lambert and his two companions entered the hall. Chester closed the door behind them, walked round to the side door, locked it, and brought the key to Lambert, who had slipped the catch on the front-door lock while he was gone.

"With my compliments," Chester said.

He ushered them into the drawing-room. Except for Susan Wareham, all the members of the party Lambert had seen on Saturday evening were there, the Lanes seated on one big sofa, Carole Boston and Hastings on another and Alethea in an easy chair. All of them looked in varying degrees puzzled and uneasy. They all had glasses, too, although only Trevor Lane appeared to have drunk from his.

"Do sit down," Chester said. "Will you have something to drink?"

"No, thank you." The Lanes' sofa was nearest the door, and Lambert perched on the arm of it beside Trevor.

Beeley moved a Victorian tub chair so that its back was to the French windows and sat in it. Flick took its twin near the other window. We might have been called here for a church meeting, she thought.

Chester was standing with his back to the fireplace. There was a glass of whisky on the mantelpiece beside him, but it was still untouched.

"Logan, why are we here?" Alethea demanded, her voice almost shrill with indignation. There was no vestige of her normal vagueness in her manner now.

"You'll soon see," Chester told her.

Trevor Lane emptied his glass, looked round for somewhere to put it, and, finding nowhere, stood it on the floor. "I don't like it," he muttered.

"I may say I don't either," Lambert agreed. Six heads turned towards him, and five pairs

294

of eyes regarded him with expressions ranging from appreciation to dull hostility. Chester merely smiled faintly.

He's enjoying himself, Lambert thought. He's holding the stage alone, and he's in his element, on such a high he hasn't even considered the possibility of danger. It's like a drug to him.

"I thought it would be a good idea for us to get together to talk about what concerns us all," Chester explained. He might have been addressing a group of reasonably bright students. "I'm sure it does concern us all, including the police." His tone hardened as he continued, "Unfortunately Susan can't be here; the person who killed Tommy attacked her and nearly killed her yesterday. Thank God they didn't succeed. And she saw who it was."

Thunder rolled again outside. Chester glanced at Lambert, who returned his gaze calmly.

It seemed to Flick she could feel the tension in the room increase. She looked at Gillian and Trevor, Alethea, and the back of Carole's head, which was all she could see of her, close to Peter Hastings'. Did Chester know anything?

"Tommy was killed between two thirty-two,

when I came in to get some drinks, and three o'clock, when Carole came to find him and the study door was locked," Chester went on.

"How do you know that?" Trevor demanded.

"There was nobody in the study when I came in because I looked in there to see if Tommy was still on the phone, and the superintendent says the post mortem confirmed he was killed between those times." Chester glanced at Carole. "I'm sorry, Carole, I know this must be horrible for you."

"I'm all right," the girl said quietly.

Hastings looked at her, then back at Chester. It seemed that none of them could take their eyes off him for more than a second or two.

"All that time," he continued, "just under half an hour, Gill, Peter and Carole were on the lawn together. I was in the kitchen. Then Susan came back and helped me with the drinks, and we took them outside. That was a minute or two after two-forty."

Lambert reflected that Chester knew Susan's watch was slow, and she hadn't returned until two forty-five. Yet he was persisting in the lie that it was five minutes earlier because that cut down the time during which he was alone in the kitchen.

Trevor didn't know, but he wasn't letting Chester get away with it so easily. "You were by yourself in there for several minutes," he said aggressively. "You could have done it."

"You think that's likely?" Chester asked him. "With Susan coming back any minute? I assure you, I had no motive, and once she returned we were together all the time. Anyway, do you think I'd have asked you all here this evening if I killed Tommy?"

"You weren't together when you went to fetch some more glasses," Lambert pointed out quietly.

There was a startled silence. Lightning flashed in the distance, and the first heavy drops of rain spattered the French windows.

"That's true," Chester conceded, apparently quite unperturbed. "I'd forgotten; I was only gone a minute or two." Nobody said anything, and after a moment he continued, "Unless Susan and I were accomplices, and I know we weren't, even if you don't, five people can be eliminated straight away: Gill, Peter, Carole, Susan and me. Which leaves two unaccounted for."

Trevor stared at him, then started rising from his seat. His cheeks were flushed with anger.

"If you think I'm going to stay here while you—" he began furiously.

"Nor will I," Alethea broke in. She had spoken more quietly, but there was no mistaking her cold fury.

"Listen!" Chester's tone was calculated to quell any protest. "The thing that stood out a mile in all this business was the way it resembled a classic detective story. It even had a locked room. The murderer must have planned it like that deliberately, to confuse things. That suggested real imagination, almost genius."

Chester looked round, but Alethea and Trevor were listening as intently as the others, and he went on, "In considering any set of facts the cardinal rules are, one, take account of them all, ignoring none, however difficult they are to fit into the pattern, and two, don't jump to conclusions. What's obvious is rarely right." Chester turned to Lambert, as if he expected to be challenged, but Lambert said nothing. "Let's take motive and opportunity then. Alethea hated Tommy."

"If you mean that ridiculous incident in the garden, it's too absurd for words," Alethea told him coldly.

"I don't—except that it reminded you of something that happened in your office some time ago. You don't want me to go into details with Carole here, do you?"

"How do you—?" Alethea began.

"I knew Victoria, remember," Chester told her. "You had motive and opportunity. You say you were in your room all the afternoon, but nobody saw you there. You could easily have waited until Susan and I took the drinks out to the garden, slipped downstairs and stabbed Tommy, and gone back up again."

"This is preposterous!" Alethea protested furiously. "If you think you can cajole me into listening to this ridiculous pantomime, you're mistaken. I'm leaving."

"I wouldn't." Chester's words cut her off like a knife. "I haven't finished yet. Now Trevor. There's another factor as important as motive and opportunity: character. Trevor's a man of action, his inclination is to hit first and ask questions afterwards. And he's apt to be jealous."

Gillian, looking worried, rested a hand on her husband's sleeve as if to restrain him, but beyond glowering at Chester, Trevor showed no reaction.

"When we were having lunch," Chester went on, addressing Trevor directly, "Tommy made a pass at Gill. I don't suppose you liked that, only she put him in his place so effectively you could afford to let it pass. Then he made out he'd read her book, and that really got under your skin because you hadn't. You weren't interested in Gill's writing, but you didn't like Tommy knowing more about her book than you did. That's why you dragged her out to the garden as soon as we'd finished lunch. And when she told you what it was about you blew up. I could see you were having a row when I came out.

"In the end you stumped off to the pub by yourself, and by the time you left with a double scotch inside you on top of the beer you'd had before lunch, several glasses of wine and a brandy, you were ready to kill anybody. I'm right, aren't I?"

You fool! Lambert thought. Was Chester so blinded by his own cleverness he couldn't see what he was doing? He tensed, ready to move fast, and out of the corner of his eye saw Beeley making a slight instinctive movement too.

But Trevor said nothing, although his anger was clear enough. "When I met you on my way to find Tommy you said you'd been to the pub, as if you'd just got back. But Bert Jarman says his last customers left by two forty-five. It was three o'clock then. What were you doing in that quarter of an hour, Trevor?"

Outside thunder crashed nearer.

17

"MIND your own bloody business," Trevor said loudly.

Flick saw that Carole and Peter Hastings were staring at Chester as if fascinated, and even Alethea looked interested.

Chester smiled. "I'll tell you what I think; I think you didn't kill Tommy." He turned to the woman in the easy chair and his voice rose a little. "Because you did, Alethea. I said whoever planned this murder possessed imagination and ruthlessness; Trevor hasn't that sort of imagination. He might have stabbed Tommy, although he'd be more likely to beat him up with his fists or a cricket bat, but he wouldn't have arranged the locked room.

"Then, a kitchen knife suggests a woman, and it would have been easy for you to hide it in that big bag of yours. You hated Tommy for what he'd done to Victoria, and when he made that pass at you in the garden it all boiled up inside you. He was repulsive, not fit to mix with people like you. You said so. Anybody getting rid of him would be performing a public service." Chester paused. "You've got the sort of brain to commit a crime like this—and however much you may pretend to despise them, you read mystery novels. You're cool, Alethea, and you're vain enough to believe you could get away with it. One other thing, the key to your bedroom is the only other key in the house that fits the lock on the study door."

Chester put his hand in his pocket. When he brought it out again the key was lying there, its metal dark against his palm, and he no longer looked triumphant but drained.

Alethea hadn't moved, but she was staring at him with a loathing frightening in its intensity.

"You!" Hastings breathed.

"Well, Superintendent," Chester said, "what are you going to do?"

Lambert didn't answer immediately. Then he said, "First of all, I'm going to tell you that most of what you've said is nonsense. What's more, if you're as intelligent as I think you are, you know it is. I warned you not to go ahead with this charade. You chose to disregard that advice, and now you'll have to face the consequences.

"When you began you said this case was like

the plot of a detective story. It isn't. But you had a reason for saying it was, just as you've had a reason for what you've done all along. Then you claimed that the obvious solution was rarely the right one, with the implication that the most likely suspect was usually innocent, and that was plain silly. You were confusing fiction with reality; in real life the person with the strongest motive is often guilty."

Chester regarded Lambert calmly, apparently not at all put out. Of all the people in the room he seemed the most at his ease. "Are you suggesting I'm the obvious suspect?" he enquired.

He had spoken lightly, but Lambert didn't miss the tension behind the words. "Aren't you?" he asked. "It was your party; you invited at least two people you knew hated Mr. Boston; you're an expert on mystery stories, so you're more likely than anybody to have thought up the trick with the locked room; and you had a motive. You'd never forgiven Mr. Boston for what he did when you had him on your programme, had you? You invited him here this weekend to get even with him, to humiliate him in front of other people."

Lambert had stood up while he was speaking,

and now, by accident or design, he was between the other people in the room and the door to the hall.

"The first thing we had to do on Saturday," he continued, "was strip away all the trimmings and look at the basic facts. Everything we were told indicated that Mr. Boston was stabbed between two thirty-two and three. Mr. Chester insisted he must have been, and, as he said just now, the post mortem confirmed that death occurred between twenty and forty minutes after you finished lunch and was virtually instantaneous. Not many of you knew exactly when you finished, but Miss Wareham had looked at the clock, and she said it was ten past two. We checked the clock and it was right. Unless somebody had tampered with it in the meantime, that seemed to show the murder was committed between two-thirty and two-fifty."

There was a crack of thunder, but it was farther away now, and the drum of rain on the French windows had eased to a gentle patter. The people in the room were watching Lambert intently, listening to every word.

"Mr. Chester was right," he went on. "That ruled out most of you, although not as conclusively as he suggested: Mrs. Boston was in here by herself for two or three minutes before she went out to the lawn, and Miss Wareham could have returned earlier than she said. But what he really glossed over was what he himself was doing, and he ignored all those facts which conflicted with the theory he put forward, or which he didn't like for some other reason.

"For example, Miss Wareham remembered afterwards that her watch was five minutes slow and she didn't get back until two forty-five. So, apart from Miss Wightman reading in her room, Mr. Chester was alone in the house for nearly a quarter of an hour. That's quite a long time to mix some fruit cup when the ingredients have been put out ready—and even when Miss Wareham came back he hadn't finished. Another thing, is he really saying Miss Wightman knew the key to her room fitted the lock on the study door? She had never been here until last week-end. Perhaps she went round the house after he told her the Bostons were coming, trying every key in turn? Then, the knife didn't come from this house, the murderer brought it with him or her. Mr. Chester had made a point of not telling anybody except Miss Wareham who his guests were to be, and he only told her about midday on

Friday." Lambert looked at Chester. "Are you suggesting Miss Wightman brought a knife with her on the off chance she might want to kill somebody while she was here?"

Chester said nothing.

"Those were, or seemed to be, the basic facts. The locked study was another. You might have expected at least one of the windows to be open on a hot day like Saturday; they were both shut and the double glazing fastened. But we were less interested in how that was done than why such an elaborate contrivance was necessary. There seemed to be only one answer, to demonstrate that the murder couldn't have been committed before two thirty-two. On the face of it it couldn't anyway, because of the time limits the post mortem had established. But when you say you finished lunch at such and such a time you mean that's when you left the table. Or, at least, when you finished eating and drinking. You didn't rush to get away on Saturday, you had coffee and brandy. That meant you must have finished eating by two o'clock at the latest, and probably a few minutes earlier.

"When we saw that it changed the whole picture. It meant Mr. Boston must have been killed between about two-fifteen and at the latest two-forty. The only person who didn't come near the house during that time was Mrs. Lane."

It was deathly quiet in that pleasant room. The storm had moved away and there was only an occasional distant rumble of thunder.

"The locked room was necessary because one of you had an alibi for after two thirty-two but not before," Lambert went on. "So much for why; what about how? That was easier, there was only one possible solution. It made no difference whether Miss Wightman's bedroom key fitted the lock, it couldn't have been used to lock the door from the outside if there was already a key on the inside, as Mr. Chester maintained and Mr. Lane confirmed. There was no way out other than by the door or the windows, and nowhere the murderer could have hidden. Yet somehow he or she had escaped from the study, leaving it sealed. Which was impossible."

Chester had perched on the arm of an easy chair. "Go on," he said. "This is fascinating."

He was trying to appear at his ease, but he couldn't conceal his tenseness, Flick thought.

Perhaps Hastings noticed it, too; he looked at him with a puzzled frown.

Lambert cursed himself for allowing Chester to manoeuvre him into this situation, so that now he had little choice but to continue. "Mr. Chester and Mr. Lane were wrong," he said. "Or, to be more accurate, one of them was mistaken, the other was lying. According to Mr. Chester, when he looked into the study just after two-thirty there was nobody there. Either Mr. Boston was still alive and staying out of the way or he was already dead. And dead men don't walk.

"Our scientists found fibres from the study carpet on the back of his jacket. It was just possible they could have got there when he fell, but when he was found he was lying on his side. Moreover the lab found other fibres which hadn't come from the study carpet, but which matched samples from one of the rugs in the hall. There were similar threads caught in the heel of one of his shoes, and a little dust on his clothes."

Lambert paused. "This case had two quite distinct phases. The first was when the murderer met Mr. Boston coming out of the study after he'd finished making his call,

309

stabbed him and dragged him into the utility room just across the hall where he wasn't likely to be found for some time since Elsie Hemmings had gone home. Long enough to make it difficult to establish exactly when he died and who was where at any given moment. Phase two started thirteen minutes later. When Miss Wareham came back she couldn't open the side door. It often stuck, so she wasn't particularly surprised, and she went round to the kitchen door. It was only later she remembered that while it usually stuck at the top, on Saturday afternoon it was in the middle. Near the lock. Yet when Mr. Lane came in a quarter of an hour after her it opened without any trouble."

"You mean somebody locked it, then unlocked it again?" Hastings asked.

"Yes," Lambert told him. "There could only be one reason for doing that, to prevent anybody coming in that way and seeing Mr. Boston's body being dragged back to the study."

"It's horrible," Carole burst out. "Dragging him about like that."

"Yes," Lambert agreed. "The person who took him back to the study locked the door on

310

the inside so that they wouldn't be disturbed, fastened both windows and the double glazing, unlocked the door again and went out, locking the door on the outside and taking the key away."

"But it was on the inside," Gillian protested.

"No, Mrs. Lane. I said a few minutes ago that when Mr. Chester and Mr. Lane said they saw it when they looked in through the window one of them was mistaken and the other was lying. I asked Mr. Lane what Mr. Chester was doing when he left him, and he said he was walking across the room towards the door. That meant he was between the window and the door, and Mr. Lane couldn't have seen the key. By then the sun was on the other side of the house and it wasn't very light in the study. Mr. Lane couldn't even see the chromium-plated letter opener on the desk, so how could he possibly have seen that dull metal key in the lock nearly twenty feet away?"

Trevor was staring at Lambert as if hypnotized.

"He assumed it was there because of what Mr. Chester told him, and because Mr. Chester unlocked the door with it to let him in," the latter went on. "That's the only way the trick can have been worked. Mr. Hastings couldn't see into the study because the other two blocked the window. Mr. Chester very reasonably asked him to call the doctor, and he came in here to use the phone. Then Mr. Chester broke the glass and Mr. Lane offered to climb in. But Mr. Chester insisted on going himself. He had to."

It seemed to Flick the atmosphere had become even more tense. Nerves were stretched taut.

"You mean Logan had the key all the time?" Hastings asked.

"Yes. He sent Mr. Lane round to the hall, put it in the lock, and opened the door to let him in. But he made two mistakes. First, he forgot to see if the other window was fastened; as soon as he found the one at the side of the house was he said they'd have to break the glass. Who would do that without checking the other window first—unless he knew that one was fastened too? Second, he was so intent on getting the key back in the lock as quickly as possible, and at the same time preventing Mr. Lane seeing what he was doing, he overlooked something else. When Mr. Lane asked him if Mr. Boston was all right he said he hadn't looked at him. Wouldn't any normal man have gone straight to him to see how he was? Unless, of course, he already knew he was dead."

Somebody gasped.

"It was a silly slip because he'd partly relied on all Mr. Lane's attention being on Mr. Boston when he looked in through the window, and not on the door."

"Logan killed Tommy?" Carole said in a stunned voice.

Lambert shook his head. "No, he was in the garden."

"But you said—" Gillian began.

Chester hadn't moved. And still he said nothing.

"He came indoors to get the drinks just after two-thirty," Lambert explained. "The freezer is in the utility-room. He went in there to get some ice, and found Mr. Boston where the murderer had left him. He dragged him into the study, arranged the sealed room, and only just got back to the kitchen before Miss Wareham came in by the kitchen door. There wasn't even time for him to unlock the side door again; he did that later when he went to get some more glasses."

"But why?" Trevor wanted to know. "Why go to all that trouble if he didn't kill Boston?"

"To confuse everything," Lambert replied. "He wanted to make the case as difficult as possible for us."

"But why?" Carole insisted, frowning.

"To protect the person he believed to be the murderer."

"Who?" Gillian breathed, staring at Chester.

"There was only one person he would go to those lengths to shield," Lambert told her. "Susan Wareham."

Nobody visibly reacted, but a kind of suppressed gasp came from them.

"Susan!" Gillian exclaimed. "I don't believe she—"

"I said the person he believed to be the murderer," Lambert reminded her. "He went into the utility-room, saw Mr. Boston's body, and his immediate reaction was that she had killed him. Miss Wightman, Mr. Hastings and Mr. Lane might have disliked him, but hardly enough to murder him. Miss Wareham, on the other hand, had really hated him. With good reason. Mr. Chester knew she hadn't needed to go to the post office, or to take the book to Miss Rider, they were excuses to get away for a little

314

while. She had followed Mr. Boston out and she was the only one he had told that Mr. and Mrs. Boston were coming for the weekend. He put two and two together—and made sixteen. Susan Wareham wasn't the murderer."

Again Lambert looked at Chester. "You realized when she was attacked yesterday, didn't you?"

Chester nodded. "Yes," he said.

It was nearly over now, Flick told herself. What would happen when it was? Her heart beat a little faster.

The old house creaked eerily, but no one in the room seemed to hear it.

"Think back to what happened after you finished lunch," Lambert went on, speaking to them all again. "First, Mr. and Mrs. Lane went out to the garden. Next Mr. Boston went to the study to make his phone call. Miss Wareham followed him, then Mrs. Boston went out the same way."

"I wanted to speak to Tommy," Carole said in a tight voice. "I was mad about the way he'd behaved at lunch, and I was going to tell him so. But he was already on the phone, so I went upstairs."

Lambert nodded. "Next Elsie Hemmings

came to say she was going home, nearly colliding with Miss Wightman who was on her way to her room. That left Mr. Chester and Mr. Hastings in the dining-room. Mr. Hastings realized he'd just got time to retrieve his pipe from the pub before it closed, and he went out the same way as the others."

"So why . . . ?" Alethea demanded.

Nobody took any notice.

"You remember what Mr. Chester said about character being as important as motive and opportunity?" Lambert asked. "In that he was right, and once you know the murderer wasn't responsible for planning the locked room you see he didn't need to possess imagination, only ruthlessness and greed. Because this was fundamentally a very simple crime. It was possible, also, that he or she had some knowledge of anatomy. Mrs. Lane's father was a doctor and she trained as a nurse for a while, and Mr. Chester has a number of medical textbooks." Lambert turned to the man sitting beside Carole. "Where were you during the first few months of 1973, Mr. Hastings?"

All eyes turned to the author. For a moment he looked startled, as if he could hardly believe what he had heard. Then he smiled. There was something repellent about that smile, Flick thought. It was appallingly smug, the smile of a man pleased with himself, whatever he had done. Almost, it seemed to her, she was seeing a part of his soul revealed.

"You know, don't you?" he said.

Lambert nodded. "On twenty-two February that year you were convicted at the Old Bailey of impersonating a surgeon at a hospital in North London and performing two operations. You asked for seven further offences to be taken into account. I must say, that seems to me one of the most cold-blooded, irresponsible crimes anybody could commit."

There was a stunned silence. Then Carole cried, "Peter, it isn't true, is it? You didn't kill Tommy?"

Hastings ignored her. Looking at Lambert, he demanded, "Why should I kill him?"

"For two reasons," Lambert told him. "First, you'd hated him ever since you started work ghosting his autobiography. You spent a lot of time at his house, and you got to know Mrs. Boston. On Saturday he went too far, talking about writing the book himself in front of you, and he added insult to injury by telling everybody at lunch it was badly written.

Second, you're very hard up. You believed Mrs. Boston would marry you if her husband was dead, and you thought she would inherit most of his estate. Once we knew the murder could have been committed before two-thirty and you had the opportunity, you were the obvious suspect, not Mr. Chester. You had the strongest motive—and the sort of character we were looking for."

"I didn't know he was going to be there," Hastings protested. "You said yourself, the only person Logan told was Susan Wareham."

"She was. But Mrs. Boston knew—and she told you when she came to see you on Thursday afternoon, didn't she?"

"Yes," Carole whispered. She had moved away from Hastings so that now he seemed isolated, everyone's eyes on him.

"You told Miss Wareham you knew there'd be trouble as soon as you heard he was coming," Lambert went on. "Not when you arrived and found he was here. You believed you could persuade Mrs. Boston not to say anything about her telling you, but Miss Wareham was another matter. So you decided to kill her too.

"When you came on Saturday you brought a

knife with you and hid it in the flower-bed by the side door. After lunch you waited until everybody else was out of the way, then you told Mr. Chester you were going to the pub to fetch the pipe you'd left there earlier. You told us you thought Elsie Hemmings was still in the kitchen because you would hardly have stabbed Mr. Boston if she was, but you knew she'd gone home by then. You retrieved your knife, came back into the house, and met Mr. Boston coming out of the study. You killed him, put his body in the utility-room and went off to the Wheatsheaf as if nothing had happened."

Nobody spoke. Hastings' right hand was in his pocket. He withdrew it and something he was holding glinted briefly in the light.

Lambert threw himself forward. As the author raised his arm he grasped it, pushed it up and back, and at the same time turning it. He heard Hastings gasp, and saw the beads of perspiration spring out on his forehead. There was an unnatural light in his eyes.

Beeley had moved at the same moment. His right arm was across Hastings' throat, forcing his head back. Another second and the knife dropped harmlessly on the sofa between the author and Carole.

"I'm going to take you to the police station," Lambert said. "There you'll be asked some further questions and be given the opportunity to make another statement if you wish to do so."

Hastings seemed to crumple. Beeley gripped his right arm and half helped, half hauled him to his feet.

"Take him out," Lambert said.

Escorted by Beeley and Flick, Hastings went out without a glance at Carole. Lambert wondered if, when they searched his house, they would find the cape and Balaclava, or if the author had already destroyed them. Even if he had, it was unlikely some remnants hadn't survived. And the forensic scientists might find more evidence when they examined his shoes and clothes.

"What will happen?" Gillian asked in a shocked voice.

"Speculation isn't my province," Lambert replied. "But almost certainly he'll be charged."

"What about the woman Susan Wareham saw outside her flat?" Flick enquired.

She and Beeley were back in Lambert's office. It was late, but none of them was

320

inclined to go home yet, although Hastings had made a new statement confessing to both crimes, and a search of his cottage had yielded the cape; Lambert supposed he had disposed of the Balaclava yesterday. Now anticlimax had brought lethargy.

"She was a Mrs. Archer," Beeley answered. "Inspector Fletcher's team turned her up. She lives round the corner, and she'd been to see her sister."

"Apparently she isn't really like Miss Wightman at all except in build and the way she does her hair," Lambert added. "But Miss Wareham only saw her back."

"If Logan Chester hadn't done everything he could to obstruct us, we might have got to Hastings before he had time to get to Susan Wareham," Flick observed soberly.

"Ironic, isn't it? His trying to protect her nearly ended up killing her. I wonder if he sees that."

Beeley snorted. "He's too damned pleased with himself. What gets me is his accusing Miss Wightman like he did. She'll crucify him." Beeley grinned at the prospect.

"He must hate her," Flick said.

"I'd say hate's too strong a word. After all,

he was ready to put up with her company for the weekend." Lambert leaned back in his chair. He had been wondering about Chester's motives and was inclined to think they were more complex than they appeared on the surface. "He certainly dislikes her; they're both far too egotistical to get on. He started off by trying to help Miss Wareham, and by the time he found she didn't need help he was enjoying himself playing detectives too much to stop. It's possible he really thought Miss Wightman was guilty. His ego's taken a pretty bad beating tonight."

"What'll happen to him?" Flick asked.

"I've no idea. He obstructed us, and I suppose he attempted to pervert the course of justice. I shall make a report, and the chief constable will decide whether to send it to the DPP's office." Lambert paused. "There's one thing I don't suppose we'll ever know."

"What's that?" Beeley and Flick asked in unison.

"Well, hasn't it occurred to you that arranging the locked room like that called for some pretty quick thinking? Almost too quick. It makes me wonder if Chester hadn't got it all worked out in advance."

"You mean . . . ?" Flick said.

"That's right. Ready for when he killed Boston," Lambert agreed. "Only Hastings got in first."

THE END

CASE WITH THREE HUSBANDS
by Margaret Erskine

Was it a ghost of one of Rose Bonner's late husbands that gave her old Aunt Agatha such a terrible shock and then murdered her in her bed? The Bonner family felt that only Inspector Septimus Finch could catch the killer.

THE END OF THE RUNNING
by Alan Evans

Lang continued to push the men and children on and on. Behind them were the men who were hunting them down, waiting for the first signs of exhaustion before they pounced.

CARNABY AND THE HIJACKERS
by Peter N. Walker

When Commander Pigeon assigns Detective Sergeant Carnaby-King to prevent a raid on a bullion-carrying passenger train, he knows that there are traitors in high positions within the railway, banking and even police circles.

TREAD WARILY AT MIDNIGHT
by Margaret Carr

If Joanna Morse hadn't been so hasty she wouldn't have been involved in the accident, and wouldn't have offered hospitality to the injured woman, only to find she was an escaped inmate from the local nursing home.

TOO BEAUTIFUL TO DIE
by Martin Carroll

There was a grave in the churchyard to prove Elizabeth Weston was dead. Alive, she presented a problem. Dead, she could be forgotten. Then, in the eighth year of her death she came back. She was beautiful, but she had to die.

IN COLD PURSUIT
by Ursula Curtiss

In Mexico, Mary and her cousin Jenny each encounter strange men, but neither of them realises that one of these men is obsessed with revenge and murder. But which one?

LITTLE DROPS OF BLOOD
by Bill Knox

It might have been just another unfortunate road accident but a few little drops of blood pointed to murder—and plunged Chief Inspector Colin Thane and Inspector Phil Moss into another adventure.

GOSSIP TO THE GRAVE
by Jonathan Burke

Jenny Clark invented Simon Sherborne because her daily gossip column was getting dull. But when the society editor demanded a picture of the elusive playboy, Jenny knew she had to get rid of him. Then Simon appeared at a party—in the flesh! And Jenny finds herself involved in murder.

HARRIET FAREWELL
by Margaret Erskine

Wealthy Theodore Buckler had planned a magnificent Guy Fawkes Day celebration. He hadn't planned on murder.

A FOOT IN THE GRAVE
by Bruce Marshall

About to be imprisoned and tortured for the death of his wife in Buenos Aires, John Smith escapes, only to become involved in an aeroplane hi-jacking.

DEAD TROUBLE
by Martin Carroll

A little matter of trespassing brought Jennifer Denning more than she bargained for. She was totally unprepared and ill-equipped for the violence which was to lie in her path.

HOURS TO KILL
by Ursula Curtiss

Margaret went to New Mexico to look after her sick sister's rented house and felt a sharp edge of fear when the absent landlady arrived. Her fears deepened into panic after she found the bloodstains on the porch.

THE DEATH OF ABBE DIDIER
by Richard Grayson

Inspector Gautier of the Sûreté investigates three crimes which are strangely connected —the murder of a vicar, the theft of a diamond necklace and the murder of Pontana's valet.

NIGHTMARE TIME
by Hugh Pentecost

Have the missing major and his wife met with foul play somewhere in the Beaumont Hotel, or is their disappearance a carefully planned step in an act of treason?

BLOOD WILL OUT
by Margaret Carr

Why was the manor house so oddly familiar to Elinor Howard? Who would have guessed that a Sunday School outing could lead to murder?

THE DRACULA MURDERS
by Philip Daniels
The Horror Ball was interrupted by a spectral figure who warned the merrymakers they were tampering with the unknown. Then a girl was ritualistically murdered on the golf course.

THE LADIES OF LAMBTON GREEN
by Liza Shepherd
Why did murdered Robin Colquhoun's picture pose such a threat to the ladies of Lambton Green?

CARNABY AND THE GAOLBREAKERS
by Peter N. Walker
Detective Sergeant James Aloysius Carnaby-King is sent to prison as bait. When he joins in an escape he is thrown headfirst into a vicious murder hunt.

VICIOUS CIRCLE
by Alan Evans
Crawford finds himself on the run and hunted in a strange land, wanting only to find his son but prepared to pay any cost.